COOKIE DOUGH AND BRUISED EGOS

AN IVY CREEK COZY MYSTERY

RUTH BAKER

CLEANTALES PUBLISHING

Copyright © CleanTales Publishing

First published in July 2022

All characters and events in this publication, other than those clearly in the public domain, are fictitious and any resemblance to real persons, living or dead, is purely coincidental.

Copyright © CleanTales Publishing

The moral right of the author has been asserted.

All rights reserved. This book or any portion thereof may not be reproduced or used in any manner whatsoever without the express written permission of the publisher except for the use of brief quotations in a book review.

For questions and comments about this book, please contact
info@cleantales.com

ISBN: 9798840246047
Imprint: Independently Published

OTHER BOOKS IN THE IVY CREEK SERIES

Which Pie Goes with Murder?

Twinkle, Twinkle, Deadly Sprinkles

Eat Once, Die Twice

Silent Night, Unholy Bites

Waffles and Scuffles

Cookie Dough and Bruised Egos

A Sticky Toffee Catastrophe

AN IVY CREEK COZY MYSTERY

BOOK SIX

1

"Is it straight?"

Lucy spared a quick glance over her shoulder at her Aunt Tricia, while concentrating on maintaining her balance. She was perched on a stepladder in front of her bakery, Sweet Delights, clutching one end of a banner with her right hand. Her left hand curled around the porch overhang in a death grip. Heights had never been her favorite thing.

"Hannah... drop your end by about an inch," Tricia suggested, standing on the front walkway with her hands on her hips, eyeing the homemade banner critically.

Lucy turned her gaze to Hannah, on a matching stepladder to her right. Hannah caught her eye and winked, before inching her side down... again.

They had been at this for a solid fifteen minutes and Tricia had still not deemed the banner straight enough. Lucy was beginning to wonder if the sidewalk her aunt was standing on was crooked.

"Perfect!" Tricia finally crowed, clapping her hands, and Lucy gratefully descended from the ladder, her knees a bit wobbly.

She joined Hannah and Aunt Tricia on the walkway, and the three of them admired their handiwork together.

SWEET DELIGHTS GRAND RE-OPENING PARTY
JOIN US AS WE CELEBRATE OUR NEW LOOK
FOOD, FUN & FRIENDS GALORE

Lucy sighed happily. "It looks great! Hannah, you did a fabulous job with the colors." Her friend and assistant never failed to amaze her with her many talents.

Hannah smiled, pleased by the compliment, and the three of them walked inside.

The bakery had undergone a massive transformation in the last month. New countertops, a fancy patterned tile flooring, and bold colors on the walls gave the interior a fresh vibe. Hidden speakers in ceiling corners piped soft music, and recessed lighting added a warm glow. The seating had doubled, with more tables downstairs, as well as an upstairs veranda where customers could enjoy their treats in the open air. Lucy had moved the office and stockrooms upstairs, into the former apartment space, and that had allowed her to expand her square footage substantially.

"I can't wait to see everyone's reactions." Aunt Tricia settled comfortably into a chair at their favorite table, next to a window overlooking the quiet street.

Lucy set down a pitcher of lemonade and poured them each a glass, while Hannah brought over a plate of cookies.

"I would say champagne is called for," Lucy said, raising a glass. "But we'll save that for the launch party. Here's to a job well done, ladies."

They clinked glasses, and Hannah snagged a cookie. Their newest recipe was called Peanut Butter Cup Crunch, and Hannah couldn't get enough of them. She nibbled and sighed blissfully. Lucy watched her with amusement.

"How is it you can eat cookies all day long and never gain an ounce?" She shook her head, marveling at her friend.

Aunt Tricia chuckled, reaching for a cookie herself. "Oh, to have a young person's metabolism again…"

The phone rang and Hannah swallowed, announcing, "I'll get it. Mrs. Fox said she would call today about her daughter's graduation cake." She pushed back her chair and dashed across the bakery.

Aunt Tricia looked around the bakery's colorful interior with appreciation. "Well, you did it. It looks fabulous, honey." She laid a hand on top of Lucy's and gave it a squeeze. "Your parents would be so proud."

Lucy smiled nostalgically, her thoughts turning to her late parents. Sweet Delights had been their life's work, and Lucy had grown up helping at the bakery. She'd moved away after high school, living in the city and working as a professional food blogger. Upon the tragic death of her parents almost two years ago, she'd decided to try running the bakery herself. Ivy Creek was her home once again, and now she couldn't imagine ever living anywhere else.

It's funny how things come full circle, she mused.

"Lucy!" Hannah called her name and Lucy turned her head. Hannah was holding the telephone, with the mouthpiece covered. Her eyes were wide as she announced in a stage whisper, "It's Richard."

Lucy froze for a minute, then stood slowly. She and Richard had dated for a few months, and though they'd never officially broken up, they had stopped seeking each other's company.

In her heart, she knew their relationship was over, and she took stock of her feelings now, walking to the phone. She really didn't feel any sadness. She'd only invited Richard to the bakery's launch party to be polite, leaving a message on his café's answering machine. She was positive he would decline, since one of the reasons they'd drifted apart was his lack of enthusiasm for her plans for expansion.

Lucy held the phone to her ear, saying cheerfully, "Good morning, Richard."

There was a beat of silence, and then she heard his familiar voice. "Hi, Lucy. How've you been?" He sounded a bit uncomfortable.

"Super! Everything turned out even better than I'd hoped. The bakery looks fabulous. I'm really excited to re-open." Lucy babbled, then made a conscious effort to stop talking.

"Yeah..." Richard sighed out a breath. "About the party. I appreciate your invitation, Lucy, but..."

Lucy waited silently, knowing what his response would be.

"I think it would be awkward," Richard blurted out. "I... really do wish you the best, you know. But I won't be coming."

Lucy nodded her head, wondering why she'd bothered to invite him. As two business owners in the small town of Ivy

Creek, she thought they should support each other... celebrate each other's successes. But apparently, Richard was not on the same page.

"OK." Lucy kept her voice emotionless. "Thanks for letting me know."

They said their goodbyes and hung up, and Lucy crossed the room to slump into her chair. *She wasn't sad*; she told herself. *Just disappointed.*

Aunt Tricia looked at her sympathetically. "He's not coming?"

Lucy shook her head and reached for a cookie. "It doesn't matter," she proclaimed. "I guess I just expected more of him." She bit into the cookie, savoring the delicious combination of flavors.

Hannah frowned, forever loyal. "He was never good enough for you. You deserve someone who will always stand by you, celebrating your victories with you... helping you get through the tough times. A real man. A partner." She took a sip of her lemonade and crunched on an ice cube.

Aunt Tricia nodded. "I agree. Like the kind of relationship your parents had. Together, through thick and thin."

Lucy shook her head ruefully, with a weak laugh. "Yes, sounds great. Does anyone know where I can find a fellow like that, here in Ivy Creek?"

As soon as the words left her lips, the bell on the bakery door jangled as it opened.

A familiar, deep voice sounded. "What does a man have to do to get a decent piece of pie in this town?"

2

*A*ll three women turned their heads, chuckling at the question. Taylor Baker, the deputy sheriff of Ivy Creek, stood in the doorway, a twinkle in his blue eyes.

Lucy grinned at him. "Hey, we're not even open for business yet!" Her voice held a teasing note as he shut the door behind himself.

She and Taylor went way back—many years ago, they'd been high school sweethearts. Even though for a while he'd seemed to hold a grudge against Lucy for leaving Ivy Creek right after graduation, in the last year, they'd become good friends again.

"I know," Taylor moaned with a pitiful expression. "I've had to resort to eating store-bought cookies while you were closed this past week."

Hannah snickered at his theatrics, and Lucy couldn't help but giggle, herself. Sweet Delights had been open during much of the renovation, but Lucy had decided to close the doors in the week leading up to the grand re-opening, both to add the final touches and build anticipation.

"Here, Taylor," Aunt Tricia patted the empty chair at the table. "Come have one of Hannah's Peanut Butter Cup Crunch cookies and tell us what you think of the new look."

Taylor didn't need to be asked twice. Lucy poured him a glass of lemonade while he sampled the bakery's newest recipe. His eyes closed reverently as he savored the sweet.

"That is *so* good…" he commented and popped the rest of the cookie in his mouth, devouring it.

He swallowed and looked around admiringly. "Wow, Lucy, this looks fantastic! And I noticed the banner out front, very nice. I bet you'll have quite the turnout. There were already a few people out on the sidewalk buzzing about the party."

"Was the banner straight?" Hannah asked with a smirk. Lucy elbowed her to keep quiet.

"You're coming, aren't you?" she asked Taylor. "And your mother?"

Taylor grinned and assured her, "Wouldn't miss it for the world."

A few minutes later he was off, declaring he had work to get back to. Lucy packed up a few cookies to tide him over and watched with a soft expression as he maneuvered through the doorway, his broad shoulders nearly filling the frame.

"Now there's a real man," Aunt Tricia commented in a low voice behind her. Lucy rolled her eyes, pretending not to hear her.

She and Taylor had already had their chance. That was in the past…wasn't it?

COOKIE DOUGH AND BRUISED EGOS

"OK, GUYS… ARE WE READY?" Lucy glanced at the clock and then peeked out through the curtain at the crowd already gathered on the sidewalk.

There were already about twenty-five people lined up, waiting for the doors to open, and the party wasn't supposed to start for another fifteen minutes. As she watched, several more cars squeezed into their parking lot, and Lucy nibbled her bottom lip nervously. *Did they have enough food?* She had only planned for about fifty attendees, sixty, max.

"We're ready!" Aunt Tricia and Hannah chorused together, and Lucy took a deep breath, opening the double doors.

The crowd surged forward, flowing like sunlight into the bakery, and Lucy greeted the townspeople, many of them by name, with a wide smile on her face. Everyone was happy, chattering excitedly, oohing and aahing over the bakery's new style. Aunt Tricia and Hannah welcomed the guests, answering questions, and offering treats and a variety of hot and cold drinks.

Platters of cookies and pastries were lined up on the countertops, each one neatly labeled, showcasing their newest creations. Sweet Delights' new "To Go" menus and business cards were strategically placed on the tables for customers to take home.

"Lucy!" A man called her name, and Lucy turned her head, not recognizing the voice. She scanned the crowd and saw a dark-haired man slowly making his way toward her, winding his way through the cluster of guests enjoying the free treats.

Recognition suddenly dawned and Lucy smiled as he reached her. "Joseph."

His green eyes flashed brightly as he grinned and shook her hand. Joseph Hiller was the town's new theater production manager, having just moved to Ivy Creek two months ago. Lucy hoped they'd be able to do business together.

"I'm so glad you could make it. Would you like a tour?"

Joseph laughed, indicating the crowd. "If you think we can squeeze through! You've had quite the turnout."

Lucy nodded, pleased that the citizens of Ivy Creek were so enthusiastic about the re-opening.

"I think we can manage. Let me show you the upstairs first. There's less of a crowd."

They shouldered their way to the staircase and Joseph snagged a lemon tart along the way. He bit into it and made a sound of appreciation. "I can see why your bakery is so popular. This is fantastic!"

Lucy glanced over her shoulder with a grin. "Thanks. That's my mom's recipe."

They wound their way upstairs and Lucy showed him her new office space and stock rooms, then led him out to the veranda. The tables were full as people chatted and enjoyed their sweets. Joseph nodded his head, admiring the view.

"Great idea! Who did you hire as a contractor? I might need to do some refreshing of the theater space… try to give it a new look. I'm afraid people will shy away because of what happened."

Lucy nodded her head, remembering how shocked the town had been months ago when the celebrated director, Pete Jenson, had been murdered on stage during a rehearsal. No wonder Joseph thought he'd need a makeover of the old theater!

She answered his questions as they made their way back down the stairs, chatting about interior decorating and budgets. As they stood together at the bottom of the staircase, Lucy's gaze landed on Taylor, who must have just arrived. He was watching her from the center of the room with a faint frown, and when their eyes locked, he made his way towards her.

"Taylor, I'm not sure if you've met Joseph?" Lucy made the introductions.

Taylor nodded stiffly; his pale blue eyes turning cold as he took the other man's measure.

Joseph quirked an eyebrow at the deputy's frosty look, then turned to Lucy, saying, "Well, I'll leave you to mingle with your guests. It's a great space, Lucy. I'll be sure to stop back in again soon."

He turned and disappeared into the crowd. Lucy shot Taylor a look, frowning.

"What was that about? Why were you so unfriendly?"

Taylor cocked his head. "Unfriendly? I wasn't unfriendly."

"Yes, you were!" Lucy insisted. "You barely grunted. Do you call that friendly?"

Taylor remained impassive. "No. I didn't say I was *friendly*. I merely stated that I was not *unfriendly*."

Lucy stared at him, exasperated. She was trying to plan a response when a woman stepped forward and cleared her throat. She looked to be in her late forties, with fading red hair shot with silver strands. She wore glasses and was dressed very conservatively, in a button-down blue dress.

She offered her hand to Lucy, saying, "I hope you don't mind my interrupting. My name is Clara Davidson. I'm Ivy Creek's librarian." She shook Lucy's hand, her cool, gray eyes studying Lucy's face.

Lucy smiled. "Lucy Hale. Pleased to meet you."

Clara nodded. "Likewise." She continued, in an urgent tone. "Miss Hale, I find myself in quite a pickle. I sincerely hope you'll agree to help me."

3

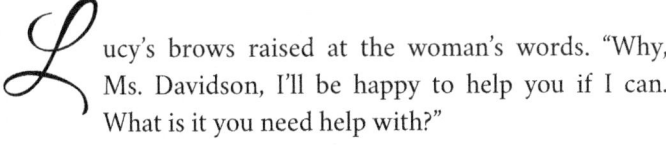ucy's brows raised at the woman's words. "Why, Ms. Davidson, I'll be happy to help you if I can. What is it you need help with?"

The librarian sighed, seeming almost embarrassed as she answered. "I know you've just re-opened your bakery, but is there any chance you could provide treats for one-hundred guests in two days' time?" With a wry twist to her lips, she explained the situation.

"You see, the town council has decided that the library will be hosting a book reading and signing by Paula Peak..." She paused, searching Lucy's face for recognition.

Lucy drew a blank and shook her head slightly. Clara sighed again.

"Paula Peak... she's an Ivy Creek local. Grew up here—though she's not in the habit of admitting it. She's a best-selling author now. Romantic suspense. *The Shadows Between Us? Behind the Garden Gates?*"

She peered at Lucy, who thought it would be prudent to just nod her head.

Clara continued, "Well, even though Ms. Peak doesn't give a *fig* about this town… for some reason—publicity most likely—she's decided to promote her new novel here. The kicker is, she'll be donating a portion of the event's sales to our Children's Hospital."

Clara snorted, her tone full of derision. "Goodness knows how her manager talked her into *that*! That woman doesn't care about anyone but herself. Regardless, the library must host the event, and *I* have been assigned to take care of all the details."

She seemed irritated, next adding, "I originally booked The Cupcake Shop in Woodboro to provide treats—as your bakery was closed recently—but there was some mix-up about the date, and they won't be able to fill the order."

She looked beseechingly into Lucy's eyes. "Is there any way you could possibly take this on, with such short notice?"

Lucy's mind spun. One-hundred guests! The contract would be near five-hundred dollars… she didn't see how she could say no to that. She may have to work into the wee hours of the morning, but…

Lucy nodded her head decisively, saying, "Yes. Yes, we can do that. Do you have a preference of what types of treats?"

Clara clasped her hands together, the picture of gratitude. "Oh, Ms. Hale, thank you so much! You have truly saved the day. Let's see, mostly cookies and brownies, and let's have some tea loaves, like banana bread and lemon pound…"

They chatted for a few minutes more, agreeing on a menu and price. Clara took her leave, promising to stop by the next day to pay for the order.

Lucy watched the woman leave, silently blessing her luck with landing such a big order immediately upon re-opening. She rubbed her hands together, itching to find Hannah and Tricia and tell them the good news.

———

Lucy and Hannah stood in the stockroom, making notes of their inventory. Yesterday's party had been a huge success, with several future orders placed on the spot—but none so impressive as Clara Davidson's order.

Even today, foot traffic was a bit more than usual, but Aunt Tricia said she could handle the counter so Lucy and Hannah could begin preparations.

"So, another fifty-pound bag of sugar, six dozen eggs… five pounds of bananas—the riper the better," Lucy dictated, closing her eyes to think.

Hannah scribbled notes on a pad. She tapped the pen thoughtfully. "Bittersweet chocolate?"

Lucy shook her head, "We have plenty. Maybe some walnuts, though. I think that will do it."

They walked together out of the supply room, and Lucy peeked over at the veranda. There were three tables occupied, and it was only eleven in the morning. She smiled, pleased at their success.

"So… Paula Peak, huh?" Hannah shook her head. "I never thought she'd come back here. I remember my mother talking about her. Apparently, her first book was a huge success, and her career took off. But her whole bio was made up."

They descended the steps together. Lucy could see Aunt Tricia was doing fine, making a latte for a young mother with a stroller.

She turned to Hannah, quizzically. "She made up her bio?"

Hannah gave a short laugh. "Yeah. Apparently, she didn't want it to be known she was a small-town girl. Claimed she grew up near Hollywood, California."

Lucy shook her head. "Wow. I bet that didn't go over well."

Hannah pursed her lips. "I don't think she has many fans in town. I hope we won't be making all this food for nothing."

Lucy shrugged helplessly. "I hope not. But, either way, it's a good sale. Clara's coming in today to pay the bill up front. She told me the town will reimburse her."

They reached the front counter just as the bell jangled, signaling another customer's arrival. Lucy turned to see who it was, not a bit surprised to see Mrs. White come in. She was a good customer, stopping by at least three days a week to buy treats for her family.

"Hello, ladies," Mrs. White greeted them all cheerfully. "I simply must have a dozen of those new cookies you had out as samples yesterday. Peanut Butter something... so delicious!"

Hannah grinned. "Peanut Butter Cup Crunch. I'll bag some up for you, Mrs. White." She flipped up the counter divider and passed through, putting on a pair of food service gloves.

COOKIE DOUGH AND BRUISED EGOS

Mrs. White looked around, marveling at Lucy. "I still can't believe you got all this accomplished in a month. It's lovely."

Lucy smiled at the compliment. "Thank you! Can we get you anything else?"

Mrs. White accepted the bag Hannah passed to her and handed over her credit card. "No, I think that should do it. I just wish I could bake these at home. You know, part of the whole enticement of a cookie is the anticipation, smelling it while it's baking. Nothing like it to make a house seem cozy."

She tucked her credit card into her purse. "Too bad you can't bottle the scent of cookies baking, Lucy. You'd rake in the dough... oh my... hahaha!"

Laughing at her own little joke, Mrs. White gave a small wave goodbye and left the store, the bell jangling behind her.

In the silence that followed, Tricia spun around to face Lucy and Hannah, her brown eyes sparkling as an idea took hold.

"Hey! Who says we can't do just that?"

4

Lucy looked at Tricia, confused. "Bottle the scent?"

Tricia shook her head, "No, sell cookie dough. I bet a lot of folks would want to bake their own cookies. As long as the recipe was yours, they'd still taste fabulous."

Hannah looked doubtful. "But wouldn't that cut into our cookie sales?"

Before Tricia could answer, Lucy shook her head, seeing the potential.

"It wouldn't hurt our profit as long as we sold the dough for almost the same price as the cookies… just marginally cheaper. Hmm." She tapped her fingers on the counter, a faraway look in her eyes.

"I think you might be onto something here, Aunt Tricia. We'd actually save money by not running the oven as much. And cookie dough freezes perfectly—we could keep a stock of each flavor in the freezer." She nodded her head, excited at the possibilities.

"Great idea, Auntie!"

Tricia smiled, looking pleased as she turned away to ring up another order. Hannah put on her apron, stating they were running low on brownies, and disappeared into the back.

Looking down at the supply list, Lucy put all thoughts of the new product line on a back burner. They had a huge order to get through first.

Right on cue, the bell jangled again, and Clara Davidson walked in, talking on her cell phone with a frown on her face.

"I don't care what Mr. Bradford told you, *I'm* telling you. That's not part of my job. You'll have to find someone else to hang your flyers." She angrily punched the hang-up button on her phone and shoved it back into her purse.

She stepped up to Lucy, and her frown disappeared. "I'm so sorry," she apologized, glancing around the store. Fortunately, there were only a few customers, and they hadn't seemed to notice.

Clara's face was still a little red, and Lucy tried to put the woman at ease.

"No worries, Ms. Davidson. How about we go upstairs to my office, and go over the contract? Can I get you something cold to drink?"

The librarian nodded gratefully. "Clara, please. Yes, some iced coffee would be lovely."

Minutes later, they were sitting in Lucy's office, with business almost concluded. Clara signed her name and handed over her credit card. While Lucy ran it through the machine, Clara leaned forward to speak earnestly.

"I do hope you'll pardon my behavior downstairs, Ms. Hale. I'm so flustered with this event being dumped in my lap."

"Lucy, please," Lucy said automatically, handing back Clara's card with a receipt. "I'm sorry. I wish there was more I could do to help."

Clara fiddled with the receipt, stashing it carefully into her purse. She snapped the purse shut, grumbling, "It's just the thought of that woman…"

"Paula Peak?" asked Lucy, her brow furrowed.

Clara looked up, her gray eyes hard. "Yes! We go way back, you know. We used to be friends… at least *I* thought so. We were in the same creative writing class, and we'd get together over drinks and discuss story ideas." Her voice drifted off as she became caught up in the memory.

"What happened?" pressed Lucy, genuinely curious.

Clara's attention snapped back to Lucy's face. "I'll tell you what happened! She stole my book idea and wrote it as her own before I knew what was going on. That's where she got her idea for her first novel. It turned into a best-seller."

Clara's face had turned red again, and Lucy searched for a way to calm her.

"Oh, I'm sure she didn't mean to… I mean," Lucy stumbled over her words. "Perhaps she didn't remember where she got the idea in the first place."

Clara glared at her, and Lucy wished she could take it back. She wasn't trying to defend Paula Peak; she was just trying to calm down Clara.

She searched for something, *anything,* to add. "Maybe you could use the experience in your own writing? As a foundation for the plot of a new book, I mean."

Clara stood up, not appeased. She waved a hand dismissively. "I don't write anymore," she informed Lucy flatly. "Thank you, Ms. Hale, for agreeing to cater the event."

With that, she turned on her heel and left, not even acknowledging Lucy as she called out her own thank you.

Lucy stared, unseeing, at the contract in front of her, shocked by Clara's accusation against the famous author. She heard the bell jangle downstairs as the librarian left and went to chat with Aunt Tricia and see what she remembered about Paula Peak.

Ten minutes later, she had convinced Aunt Tricia to take a break, and had just finished relaying the conversation.

Tricia sipped at her iced latte. "Mmm, mmm, mmm," she said, shaking her head.

"Well, I'll have to say, that doesn't surprise me. You know, when Paula's first novel made the New York Times Bestseller list, a lot of us here in town were so excited and proud. And then she went on TV and did her first interview. I remember watching it myself. Talking all about her glamorous upbringing on the West Coast." Aunt Tricia looked indignant at the memory. "Flat out lies! Like she was too good for Ivy Creek all of a sudden. Word got out around town, and they even pulled her book from Red's Corner Store. No, Paula Peak doesn't have any friends in this town."

"But do you think she stole Clara's book idea?" asked Lucy.

Aunt Tricia shrugged. "Honey, there's no way to really know, is there? It doesn't matter now, that woman has, what? Four or five best-sellers under her belt these days?"

She patted Lucy's hand. "Don't get yourself all worked up about this. Just cater the event and be done with it. It's not likely Paula Peak will stay in Ivy Creek a moment longer than she has to."

Just then, Hannah came clattering down the stairs after tidying up the veranda dining area.

"Lucy, I found Clara Davidson's credit card on the floor outside the office." Hannah held up the card. "She must have dropped it."

Lucy sighed. She'd better return the card immediately.

"OK. Aunt Tricia, could you call her at the library, please? I've got to run out and buy some supplies. I'll drop by the library and return it while I'm out."

Aunt Tricia agreed, and Lucy grabbed her purse, tucking the card inside.

Maybe while she was there, she could smooth things over with Clara. It bothered her that the woman had left the bakery in such an irritated state.

Lucy thought about how she would feel in Clara's shoes if what the librarian was saying was true.

Would she be able to hold her tongue when surrounded by the adoring fans of Paula Peak? Or would she use the opportunity to cause a scene and make her accusations public?

As Lucy drove away from Sweet Delights, she couldn't help but wonder if she'd made a huge mistake in agreeing to take part in the event.

5

Lucy loaded the supplies into her SUV, pleased that she'd managed to talk the owner of Bing's Grocery into giving her a bulk order discount. The way things were starting to boom at Sweet Delights, it made sense to buy her supplies on a larger scale, and she'd rather shop locally if she could.

Across the parking lot she saw a man on the cobblestone walkway in front of the shops stapling flyers to the posts that lined the street. A few people waiting for the bus wandered over to read them.

Curious, Lucy shut the hatch of her vehicle and walked over. Just as she approached, a man reached out and ripped the flyer down, crumpling it into a ball and tossing it into a waste can.

"We don't need her kind around here!" He complained to his companion, who nodded her head as they walked away together.

Lucy had a sinking feeling in her stomach as she stepped over to another post sporting the same flyer. Her suspicions were confirmed. It was an advertisement for the book signing at the library tomorrow. Her mood plummeted, as she realized the event probably wouldn't be well attended. Even though she'd be paid regardless, she'd still hoped Sweet Delights would benefit from the exposure.

A woman stepped up beside Lucy, reading the flyer out loud. "Award winning local author Paula Peak, reading from her new novel, *Destiny's Pathway* at the Ivy Creek Public Library at 2 P.M. Book signing to follow."

"Hmm." She glanced up at Lucy. "You ever read any of her books?"

Lucy shook her head. "No, but Sweet Delights Bakery will provide free treats." She added, "That's my bakery."

The woman looked impressed. "Wow, really? I've heard of you guys. Maybe I'll go, just to try some samples." She glanced back at the flyer. "They really should mention that. People love free food." She offered Lucy a smile and went on her way.

Lucy privately agreed, wondering why the flyer hadn't mentioned it. It would be such a good PR opportunity for the bakery, if only the event was well attended. It was probably too late to have the info added to the flyers, but maybe the library could hang out a banner... kind of like the one Hannah had made for the launch party.

She wasn't sure if she should approach Clara with the idea, given her mood about the event. She decided to wait and see if the librarian was in a more receptive state of mind.

She got back into her car, and within minutes she was parking in the library's shady lot, noticing there were only two other cars.

The library was cool and quiet. It was an older building, and as Lucy passed through its weathered wood hallways, she thought of all the people who had come here before her. Generations of Ivy Creek citizens, young and old.

Lucy loved books, the smell of them, the feel as you turned the pages, the idea of words printed long ago standing the test of time. She'd heard speculation that print books would someday be a thing of the past, since e-books were becoming so popular, and she thought if that day ever arrived, it would be a very sad day indeed.

She entered the main area and, seeing the desk was unattended, called out a hello.

"Ms. Davidson?" Lucy's voice echoed back to her, and she immediately winced, expecting someone to shush her.

There was no response, so Lucy wandered a bit, seeing a chair pulled out from a table with a man's cap and jacket resting upon it. There was an upper level to the library, so she assumed the owner of the garments was browsing titles.

She backtracked to the hallway, finding the office. The door was locked. Across the hallway, there was a single restroom, and she could see a sliver of light spilling out underneath the door. *Perhaps that's where Clara was.*

She strolled down the long hallway, all the way to the end, admiring the framed prints of historic Ivy Creek buildings that were hung at intervals. Coming to the end of the corridor, she spied a door marked *Employees Only*. Light showed underneath this door, as well.

Lucy stopped, wondering if she should knock, or just go back to the front desk. After all, Clara was sure to return to her post, eventually.

As she stood, undecided, there was a sudden rattling sound, like the door was being jiggled. Next came a thud, a female voice muttering something unintelligible, then a screeching sound of protest as the door was slowly opened.

Lucy stepped back, startled, blinking at Clara Davidson.

The librarian seemed surprised to see her, as well.

She took in Lucy's puzzled expression and stepped away from the door, revealing a glimpse of a rather outdated restroom.

Chuckling, Clara said, "It's quite an adventure getting this door to open in the humid weather. It sticks so hard; you'd swear you were trapped. Just a lock plate issue; you need to jiggle the handle and pull it sideways. I keep meaning to get it fixed. Old building, you know."

Clara shut the door behind herself, and Lucy regained her composure, noticing the woman seemed to have gotten over her irritation. *Thank goodness.*

"Ms. Davidson, I'm here to return your credit card. Hannah found it on the carpet outside my office." Lucy smiled apologetically, fishing the card from her pocketbook, and handing it over.

Clara waved her hand. "Please, call me Clara. Yes, I was expecting you. Someone called from the bakery. Thanks so much for bringing it over... it must have slipped out of my purse."

They walked together down the hall, and Lucy debated whether she should bring up her idea of a banner. As they approached the end of the corridor near the office, an older man exited the public restroom, heading back to the library's main room.

Clara addressed Lucy. "I apologize for my bad temper earlier. It was nothing to do with you. I had just had an argument with Paula Peak's manager, and I guess I was still irritable."

Lucy offered a smile, saying, "Oh, please, no need to apologize. I understand." She recalled Clara's words upon entering the bakery. "Was it having to do with the flyers? I just saw them being posted around town."

Clara made a face. "Yes. Ms. Peak's manager, Mr. Barclay, told me a town council member volunteered my services to distribute them." She sniffed. "That is definitely outside the parameters of my duties as town librarian, so I said no."

Lucy was quiet for a moment, thinking it would be unwise to bring up the banner, all things considered. "I hope we have enough of a turnout that all the food gets eaten," she said lightly.

Clara assured her, "Oh, believe me, there won't be a morsel left. Mr. Barclay informed me he's arranged to bring in a busload of Paula Peak fan club members." Her lips twisted wryly. "I believe we'll be packed to the gills."

Lucy raised her eyebrows at the disclosure. There was a lot of cost and effort going into this event, ensuring it would be worthy of news coverage. *A lot of publicity for Paula Peak... and Sweet Delights, as well - if she was lucky.*

Tomorrow was certainly going to be an interesting day.

6

Lucy and Hannah worked long into the night, leaving the bakery at one in the morning to catch a few winks, before returning four hours later. Their hard work paid off. By late morning, every possible surface in the bakery was overflowing with trays of pastries and cookies, the counters stacked high with platters of cinnamon rolls and sticky buns. Loaves of assorted tea breads were sliced and wrapped alongside tiny tubs of butter and cream cheese.

In the back, the work area was a disaster zone. Flour dusted the floor and tables; drips of batter splashed the mixer tables. There were stray berries rolling on the floor, waiting to be squashed underfoot, and the sink was overflowing with dirty dishes.

Lucy and Hannah stood in the doorway, eyeing the mess, dispirited and exhausted. Hannah stifled a yawn, rolling her neck.

Lucy sighed. "OK," she said, rolling up her sleeves. *It wasn't going to clean itself up.*

Aunt Tricia suddenly appeared at her elbow, shooing them both out.

"I'll take care of this. You girls have worked all night. Go home and get off your feet for a bit."

Hannah looked at Lucy hopefully.

"Really?" Lucy asked Tricia. "You don't mind?" She really needed some down time. She planned to stay for the entire book signing event, hoping to get a few bakery orders.

"I insist," replied Tricia firmly, and it was settled.

Lucy and Hannah went their separate ways, with Hannah agreeing to meet her at the library in time to unload the baked goods from the van. Lucy drove back to the house she shared with Aunt Tricia, and spent the next hour relaxing, cuddled on the couch with her white Persian cat, Gigi.

Too soon, it was time to get up and moving. Gigi followed her into the bathroom, watching through the glass pane of the shower door, meowing her distrust of the water cascading over her favorite human. Lucy talked to the cat as she bustled about getting ready, feeding Gigi her breakfast before grabbing her keys and heading for the door.

"Wish me luck," she called to Gigi, shutting the door behind herself.

AS LUCY PULLED into the library's small parking lot, the first thing she noticed was the bus. Dozens of chattering Paula

Peak fans were exiting the vehicle, looking around excitedly. The other parking spaces were filling up, too, and Lucy was happy to realize the event would be well-attended.

But that did create another issue. The line of fans spiraling through the lot wound across the prime parking spaces right in front of the building, where Lucy had hoped to park. She had just rolled down the van's window, hoping to catch someone's attention, when she heard a familiar voice.

"OK, people, if you could all step over here... the food has arrived!" Taylor directed the crowd with a sweep of his arm, and caught Lucy's eye, giving her a wink. Seeing him in his element, authoritative and helpful, made her smile. She gave him a wave and backed into the space. As she exited the van, Hannah came trotting over. *Perfect timing.*

Fifteen minutes later, under Clara's direction and the appreciative regard of those already inside, Lucy and Hannah had distributed the trays of goodies all around the main room.

"Oh, that's just delicious," Clara complimented Lucy, after taking a bite of banana bread spread lavishly with cream cheese. She patted her lips primly with the napkin which had the Sweet Delights Bakery logo printed on it in pink and black.

"Thank you," Lucy accepted the compliment with a smile. "It's an old family recipe."

People milled about, nibbling sweets and talking, clustered in small groups. Some already sat in the metal folding chairs that had been set up to face a small podium. There was a table at the front of the library which held stacks of Paula Peak's new novel, *Destiny's Pathway*, with an empty desk and chair next to it, where Lucy presumed the book signing would take place.

She glanced at her watch, wondering when the famous author would make her appearance.

"She'll most likely be late," she heard Clara mutter. "Dramatic entrance and all."

No sooner had the words left the librarian's lips than there was a commotion at the entrance, and a woman strode into the room with regal bearing. *Paula Peak*. Her hair was a brassy blonde, twisted up on top of her head in a sophisticated style. She wore a copper-colored silk pantsuit, with flared sleeves and a plunging neckline, showcasing a large, ornate, copper and gold pendant, set with citrine gemstones.

She paused dramatically at the sight of the crowd, pressing her hands to the base of her throat, palms crossed, in a pantomime of gratitude. Cell phone cameras caught the pose, the flashes from photo-snapping fans competing with the diamonds glittering on her fingers.

"My loyal fans…" she held both hands out next, encompassing the room. "I am delighted you could make it."

The crowd responded with a smattering of applause, and people hurried to find their seats.

Lucy studied the woman's heavily made-up face, noticing despite her gracious words, the deep frown lines and hard set of her mouth lent Paula Peak a jaded, dissatisfied expression.

Movement at the entrance caught her attention, and Lucy turned to see two gentlemen entering the room, making a beeline for Paula.

Clara nudged Lucy, saying, "The calvary has arrived. Come, let me introduce you."

They approached the trio just in time to hear Paula complain to the man on her right, a tall fellow in his fifties who wore an impeccable, blue pinstripe suit.

"Geoff, I specifically told you I needed the Cartier pen! Don't you ever hear a word I say?" She sighed, exasperated, and the man tried to soothe her, holding out a silver pen.

"Now, Paula, this one will work perfectly fine... do you really think your fans will notice what pen you're using?" His words were delivered in a light tone, but Paula scowled, turning her back to him, and he shook his head, tucking the pen away into his breast pocket.

The other man acknowledged their approach, swiping a somewhat rumpled black fedora from his head.

"Ah... Ms. Davidson, I presume?" His dark eyes darted back and forth between Clara and Lucy, unsure of which of them to address. His suit was wrinkled, his necktie loosened, and his skin had an oily sheen. *He was either very nervous or very warm*, Lucy thought.

Clara's voice held a touch of frost as she looked down her nose at the man. "Mr. Barclay, is it?" *The manager who asked her to hang flyers*, realized Lucy.

He nodded his head, crumpling the rim of his hat as he twisted it in his hands.

Clara addressed the trio, her eyes flicking over each of them in turn.

"I want to introduce the woman behind all the delectable goodies." She inclined her head toward Lucy. "This is Lucy Hale, owner of Sweet Delights Bakery."

Lucy smiled hello, and Paula turned to her, regarding her curiously.

"You own that bakery? I remember, years ago, Sweet Delights was owned by a married couple."

Lucy nodded. "Yes, that was my parents. I took over the bakery when they died."

Paula shook her head incredulously. "I cannot imagine why you would want to chain yourself to this godforsaken town."

With a harsh bark of laughter, she turned and walked away, leaving Lucy stunned, staring after her, speechless.

The man in the suit huffed out a sigh. "Please excuse my wife," he said, his blue eyes meeting Lucy's. His face showed a mix of weariness and exasperation. "She's under a lot of pressure with the book tour."

Lucy exhaled a breath, letting the negativity go. She offered him a smile. "I understand, Mr. Peak. We're just grateful to have Ivy Creek included as a stop on the book tour."

The man's face darkened, his smile vanishing. "My name is Farnsworth, Ms. Hale. Geoff Farnsworth. Peak is my wife's pen name."

Lucy turned red, apologizing instantly. "I'm so sorry! I just thought…"

Geoff waved away her concern, though he still appeared irritated. "It happens all the time. As my wife is fond of reminding me, Paula Farnsworth doesn't have the same ring to it."

Lucy smiled slightly, unsure of what to say.

Fortunately, she was saved by a sudden screech of feedback from the microphone. All eyes swiveled to the podium, where Paula Peak stood waiting for quiet.

The reading was about to begin.

7

"As the fog lifted, Jacqueline searched the horizon, realizing that she was now completely alone on the island." Paula closed the book and looked up expectantly.

There was a beat of silence, and then the crowd burst into enthusiastic applause. Paula stepped to the side with a sweeping bow. Lucy had to admit, the reading had left her intrigued, and she was tempted to purchase a copy of the book herself.

Paula stepped down from the podium and Stan Barclay took her place, reminding everyone that *Destiny's Pathway* was available for purchase, and that Paula would be signing copies near the front desk in five minutes.

Lucy walked over to a table of refreshments, selecting a bottle of water. She was joined by Hannah, who had been seated at the back.

"Wow, that was great," Hannah commented. "She got me hooked after only one chapter."

Lucy agreed, her eyes roaming over the crowd. The treats from the bakery had been a huge hit, and she was pleased to notice several folks pocketing the business cards she had strategically placed.

Activity in the far corner of the room suddenly drew her attention. Paula and Stan were faced off in the midst of what seemed to be a heated argument. Paula appeared to be furious with her manager, who was holding his hands palms up, trying to calm her down. She hissed a final comment at him and stomped away.

Lucy couldn't help but feel sorry for the man, as he rubbed the back of his neck, looking dejected. She got the feeling Paula Peak was not an easy client to have.

"Did you see that?" Hannah whispered, and Lucy nodded. "Seems our author has a bad temper."

Lucy suddenly noticed Clara waving, signaling to her from the center of the room where she stood with Geoff. At that moment, Paula walked up to join her husband.

"Do you want to meet the author?" she asked Hannah.

"Sure!"

Together, they approached the trio, finding Clara looking pleased as she observed the bustling crowd.

"Ms. Hale," began Geoff, after nodding at Hannah. "I just wanted to say thank you for providing the treats for today's event. Everyone certainly seems to be enjoying them."

Lucy beamed. "Thank you so much for the opportunity," she replied. She indicated Hannah. "This is my assistant, Hannah Curry."

"Hello," Geoff said, then glanced over at Paula, who was looking away, a bored expression on her face. "Ms. Hale, as a thank you, my wife would like to offer you an autographed copy of *Destiny's Pathway*. Complimentary, of course."

Lucy smiled graciously, turning to Paula. "Why, thank you. It was a very intriguing first chapter, Ms. Peak."

Paula glanced at Lucy, baring her teeth in what didn't quite pass for a smile. She turned her head to address Clara with a frown.

"Doesn't this building have a private restroom? Surely you don't expect me to stand in line with *those* people?" She inclined her chin toward the people waiting outside the small public restroom.

Clara assured her, "Oh, no, of course not. Follow me." She led Paula away, winding through the crowd. Lucy noticed a few fans clamoring for the author's attention, but Paula ignored them all.

Stan joined them next, questioning Geoff anxiously. "Where's she going? She's supposed to be signing books from 2:30 to 3:15."

Geoff waved a hand. "Just the restroom. She'll be back in a few minutes."

Lucy introduced Hannah to Stan, and the four of them made small talk while they waited for Paula to return. Clara had resumed her position at the front desk, tending to the sales of the book. There was a line of people already waiting in front of the author's signing table, the line getting longer as the minutes ticked by.

Stan looked at his watch, grimacing. "Geoff..." he began.

Geoff looked annoyed. "Yes, yes, I know. I'll go see what the delay is." He looked over at Clara, who was busy ringing up sales, then glanced down at Lucy and Hannah.

"I don't suppose either of you know where the private restroom is?"

Lucy nodded, pointing. "Just go to the entrance and follow the corridor to the left. It's all the way down at the end of the hall, on the right."

Geoff nodded his thanks and walked away.

Stan looked at the ever-growing line of fans waiting, and shook his head, his fingers twitching as he hooked his thumbs in his pants pockets. He cleared his throat and asked Lucy.

"So… how's the bakery business here? Lucrative?"

Lucy opened her mouth to answer, but just then a friendly hand was laid on her shoulder. She turned her head to see Taylor smiling down at her.

"You've outdone yourself, Lucy. Everyone is talking about the fantastic pastries! Wise move, putting your business cards out. I've seen a lot of people pick them up."

Lucy smiled at his praise. "Thanks! Taylor, this is Mr. Stan Barclay, Paula Peak's manager. Mr. Barclay, this is Taylor Baker, the deputy sheriff."

Stan was in the middle of shaking Taylor's hand when he heard the man's title. He froze for just a split second, but regained his composure almost instantly. Lucy saw from Taylor's expression that he, too, had noticed the man's hesitation. He narrowed his eyes at Stan, though he kept his easy grin in place.

"Pleased to meet you, Mr. Barclay... ever been to Ivy Creek before?"

Stan fidgeted, slicking a hand over his hair, and pulling at his tie. He shook his head with a forced smile, his gaze flicking from Taylor to Lucy to Hannah.

"Nope. Can't say that I have."

Just then Geoff strode through the crowd, seeking Lucy.

"Ms. Hale, could you show me where that restroom is? I don't know if I found the right door." Geoff glanced over at the line of fans waiting for their books to be signed. They seemed to be getting impatient. "The door had an *Employees Only* sign on it, but it didn't say restroom... and the door was locked. I knocked, but there was no answer."

Lucy frowned. That was odd. Paula hadn't come back, so she must still be in there. She glanced over at Clara, but saw the librarian was too busy to bother.

Taylor saw her frown. "What's the matter?" he asked in a low tone.

Lucy shook her head at him. "I'm sure it's nothing." She addressed Geoff. "Sure. I'll come with you. Maybe she didn't hear you knock."

"Where is she? Where's Paula?" asked Stan, sounding worried. "Did she leave the building?"

Geoff ignored his question, turning away. Lucy felt Taylor at her elbow as they made their way across the library. She was sure nothing was wrong, but she took comfort in his presence. Hannah trailed after them.

They entered the corridor, their footsteps echoing as they made their way down to the end, far from the animated crowd. Taylor glanced at the historic photos on the walls with a sound of surprise.

"I've never been down this hallway. You say there's a restroom down here?"

Lucy nodded. "Yes. It seems very old. The door is marked, *'Employees Only'*."

They arrived at the door, and Lucy could see the light peeking out underneath. She looked at Geoff, her hand poised to knock. He nodded.

She rapped on the door lightly. "Ms. Peak? Are you in there?"

Silence. Lucy knocked harder. "Hello? Are you in there, Ms. Peak?"

Taylor bent to examine the doorknob. "No keyhole." He twisted the knob. It was locked.

He looked at Geoff and Lucy while Hannah hung back, nervously chewing her lip.

"I'm beginning to have a bad feeling about this," Taylor muttered, his voice grave.

He pounded on the door. "This is Taylor Baker, with the Ivy Creek Police Department. I need you to open the door, please."

Collectively, they held their breath. Not a sound could be heard. The back of Lucy's neck prickled with growing dread.

Taylor pounded the door again, then warned the others, "Step back."

In a loud voice, he said, "This is the Ivy Creek Police Department. Step away from the door. I'm coming in!"

He kicked the door once, twice, and the old hinges gave out, the door hanging crookedly. Taylor pulled it away from the frame.

They all stared in horror at the scene before them.

Paula Peak lay motionless on the restroom floor, a blueish cast to her face, her hands clutching at her throat. A few crumpled paper towels were scattered around her.

"Call 911!" Taylor shouted.

Geoff fumbled with his phone as Taylor rushed forward to kneel at the author's side, checking for a pulse.

His eyes connected with Lucy's.

"She's dead."

8

Geoff dropped his phone with a clatter. "No!" he cried, rushing forward. Taylor stopped him with an outstretched arm.

"I'm sorry," he said. "I need you to stay back." He glanced up at Lucy, and she got the message.

She came forward, taking hold of Geoff's arm while Hannah picked up the dropped phone, walking away to talk into the receiver. Lucy guided Geoff back into the hallway, where he wept into his hands, his shoulders shaking with silent sobs.

"They're on their way," Hannah said, her voice trembling a bit. She looked white as a ghost.

Taylor didn't look up from his inspection of the fallen woman. "Hannah, please tell Ms. Davidson to clear the library. Tell her she can say the author has taken ill."

Hannah left immediately to do his bidding, while Geoff slumped against the wall, sliding down until he was sitting on the floor, his head cradled on his knees.

Lucy stepped forward, noting the blue pallor on the author's face. "Did she choke on something?" she asked, puzzled. *But on what, alone in a restroom?*

Taylor didn't answer immediately, turning the woman's head and seeming to examine something on her neck. He glanced sharply around at the room next, and Lucy followed his gaze upward.

A small window was set high on the opposite wall. The torn screen waved softly in the breeze.

Taylor gently rolled the body on its side, seeming to be searching for something.

"Aha," he murmured, scooting something out from under the corpse.

A bee. A very large bee.

"Mr. Peak," Taylor addressed the grieving man, and Lucy cringed at the error.

"Mr. Peak, was your wife allergic to bee stings?"

The man raised his head, his eyes streaming with tears, his face mottled with red splotches. He stared mutely for a moment, then comprehension seemed to dawn. He wiped at his face with a shaking hand and nodded.

"Is that how she died?" he asked, incredulous. "But how… how did… we're inside!"

Lucy was stunned. *A chance bee sting and Paula Peak was dead?* She couldn't wrap her mind around it.

Taylor answered Geoff. "We won't know until the coroner gets here, but it looks like anaphylactic shock. There's a large welt on her neck... and a dead bee beneath her. Was she severely allergic?"

Geoff nodded. "She won't even do any outside events, only indoor. It's in her contract." His voice shook, and Lucy's heart squeezed for him.

"Didn't she carry an EpiPen?" Taylor asked, his brows drawing together.

Geoff's eyes filled with tears again. "It's in the glove box of our car." He began to weep again, just as paramedics arrived, accompanied by two more officers.

Taylor looked at Lucy. "Lucy, could you please bring Mr. Peak back out to wait in the library office?"

She nodded, still in a state of shock herself, and led Geoff away.

Another terrible tragedy in Ivy Creek, just when things were finally getting back to normal.

Hours later, Lucy rested her chin in her hands, looking at Aunt Tricia across the bakery table.

"I still can't believe it," she admitted, finished with relaying the shocking turn of events. The flurry of baking early this morning seemed light years away.

Aunt Tricia shook her head in disbelief. "So, did you say Taylor took her husband into custody?"

Lucy frowned. "Not exactly. He just asked Mr. Farnsworth to come down to the station. I think he just had some questions."

"Like why she didn't have the EpiPen on her?" Aunt Tricia mused.

Lucy considered, tilting her head. "Well, it *was* an indoor event."

"Still... if she was that allergic, you'd think she'd always carry it on her."

Lucy thought back to her first impressions of the author, in her silk pantsuit, adorned with jewelry. "Honestly, I don't remember her even carrying a purse. And given what she was wearing... well, there wouldn't be any way to carry it on her."

Lucy sighed. "It's a shame she chose to use that old restroom. Private, yes, but obviously in need of repairs, what with the ripped window screen and the door..."

She suddenly stood up straight in her chair, eyes wide. "The door! I'd forgotten about the door. Yesterday Clara said it sticks so bad you feel like you're trapped inside, you have to wiggle it... something about the lock plate..." She stood and headed for the telephone.

"Who are you calling?" asked Tricia, confused.

"Taylor," Lucy answered. "He needs to know about the door sticking. Maybe Paula felt like she was locked inside. It would explain why she didn't come running out."

Within minutes, Taylor's brisk hello sounded in her ear. Lucy quickly relayed what she knew about the restroom door, adding that she'd been so shocked earlier that she'd forgotten all about it. Taylor listened patiently, adding "hmm" and "uh-huh" a few times during the telling. When Lucy was finished, he gave her some news of his own.

"Well... that is helpful, Lucy, thanks. But what I'm focused on now is how the bees got in there."

"Bees?" asked Lucy, frowning. She thought there had been only one bee.

Taylor informed her, "There were eight. Most of them were stuck under her clothing. She had welts all over her body."

The blood drained from Lucy's face. "Oh, that poor woman! And she couldn't get away..." Then she realized what Taylor had said. "What do you mean, "how" they got in there? The window screen was ripped."

Taylor sighed. "Yes, but what are the odds of eight bees coming through a ripped screen at the exact time a highly allergic person is using that restroom?"

It did sound improbable, but not impossible, Lucy thought.

"But how else would they have gotten in there?" she asked, puzzled.

Taylor replied. "I don't know, Lucy. But I plan to investigate all possibilities, including foul play."

Lucy nodded mutely, absorbing the information, as Taylor continued.

"I'm glad you called. If you don't mind, I'd like for you to come down to the station tomorrow and give me your official statement."

9

"... *And* that's when he came back and told me he wasn't sure if he had the right door." Lucy finished. "You were standing with us by then."

Taylor steepled his hands on the desk, pondering. "So, you estimate Mr. Farnsworth was only gone for five minutes after he went to check on his wife?"

Lucy nodded. "She had already been gone for almost fifteen minutes by then."

Taylor pursed his lips. "Do you recall seeing anyone follow Ms. Peak when she left to go use the restroom?"

Lucy thought back. "I don't think I was really paying attention. Clara escorted her, and I was talking to Mr. Barclay and Hannah."

"Was Mr. Barclay with you the whole time Ms. Peak was gone?"

Lucy nodded. "He seemed very anxious that she was making people wait to have their books signed." She thought back on

Stan Barclay, and his fidgeting. He seemed to be anxious in general… just one of those nervous types, she supposed.

Taylor leaned forward. "I have a statement from another individual who says that Mr. Barclay and Ms. Peak were involved in a heated argument directly after the reading. Did you witness anything like that?"

Lucy nodded. "Yes. Paula seemed very angry with him."

"Did you hear what it was about?"

Lucy shook her head. "They were too far away." She studied Taylor's face, noting his furrowed brow. "Do you think she was murdered?" She couldn't see how, herself. *Bees were unpredictable… how do you make someone get stung?*

Taylor sighed. "I'm not at liberty to discuss the details of the case with you, Lucy, you know that. But I will say we haven't ruled the death as an accident yet."

He stood up, and Lucy did the same, smoothing her skirt.

Taylor chuckled weakly, with no humor in the sound. "Once again, you seem to be present when a dead body turns up… how exactly does that work?"

Lucy glanced at his face, shaking her head ruefully. "I have no idea. I wouldn't mind a bit if it never happened again, though."

They said their goodbyes at Taylor's office door, and Lucy turned to leave. As she walked through the station, she heard an officer call out to Taylor.

"Deputy Baker, that entomologist called back. Says he can be here in an hour."

COOKIE DOUGH AND BRUISED EGOS

Back at the bakery, Lucy threw herself into her work, trying to put Paula Peak's death behind her. She was convinced it was just a bizarre accident, and she tried not to dwell on how awful the woman's final moments must have been, stuck in the restroom, unable to escape the bees.

She steered her thoughts, instead, to the details of their new product line: take-and-bake cookie dough.

"Six flavors would be perfect," she told Hannah, ticking them off on her fingers. "Obviously, chocolate-chip, since it's a classic. Then I was thinking, oatmeal-raisin, gingersnap, lemon sugar cookies… and… what else?"

"Peanut Butter Cup Crunch," Hannah said promptly, with a grin, and Lucy laughed.

"OK, yes. One more…" she pondered the choices. "Snickerdoodle?"

Hannah tilted her head. "Too boring. Chocolate Peanut Butter Chip?"

Lucy shook her head. "Only one peanut butter flavor."

Hannah screwed up her face, thinking. "Butter Toffee Caramel?"

"Perfect!" Lucy scribbled it on her pad. "Let's go look at the stockroom. The event at the library wiped us out of a lot of ingredients."

They climbed the stairs together, and Hannah stopped at the top, turning to face Lucy.

"I told Taylor I saw Mr. Barclay and Ms. Peak arguing." She looked apprehensive. "He seemed pretty interested. Do you think Paula was murdered?"

"By bees?" Lucy scoffed. "No, I don't. And don't forget, Mr. Barclay was with us the whole time she was in the restroom. There was no way he could have trapped her in there with the bees."

They entered the stockroom, and Lucy continued. "I think it was just a bizarre accident. Unfortunate, but an accident, nonetheless."

Hannah sighed. "I sure hope you're right. This town has seen enough murders in the last few years."

"Murders?" Aunt Tricia popped her head in. "Are they saying Paula Peak was murdered?" She had a rag and bottle of sanitizer in her hands, and Lucy assumed she'd been cleaning off the veranda tables.

Lucy assured her. "No, although Taylor said they haven't ruled her death as an accident yet. I think the investigation is just a formality, given the bizarre circumstances."

Aunt Tricia shook her head. "Who would have thought? A few bee stings and her life is cut short. I never knew bees were so dangerous."

"Neither did I," chimed in Hannah. "My cousin is allergic, and carries an EpiPen, but she told me once, even if she were stung and didn't have it with her, it was pretty unlikely it would be fatal. She might have trouble breathing, though."

"Maybe Paula was more severely allergic? Plus, she was stung several times," Lucy reasoned. "From the look on her face, she suffocated." She tried to banish the image of Paula's blue-tinged face from her mind, shuddering.

Aunt Tricia shut her eyes, shaking her head. "That poor woman. No matter that she might have been a bit snobby about her roots. No one deserves to die that way." She turned and left the stockroom, and Lucy heard her descending the stairs.

Lucy turned back to her notepad. "OK, it looks like we might need some brickle bits, butter, raisins and more flour."

Hannah rolled her eyes. "More flour? We just bought fifty pounds."

Lucy shrugged. "We got pretty wiped out with the library contract. Do you want to go to town, or shall I?"

Hannah thought for a moment. "There's a baby shower cake that needs to be decorated. I'd rather take that on."

"Deal," said Lucy instantly. She knew Hannah was more skilled at cake decorating, and besides, she'd only dwell on the circumstances of the author's death if she was stuck in the bakery.

"Be careful out there," Hannah admonished, and Lucy nodded with a sober expression.

There were hidden dangers in Ivy Creek that she'd never imagined.

10

As Lucy entered Bing's Grocery, she noticed a new display had been set up at the front of the store. Stacks of *Destiny's Pathway* were set in front of a large sign, reminding shoppers the novel was written by "Local Author Paula Peak". Several people were flipping through copies, reading the back cover, and others huddled in groups, discussing yesterday's shocking news in hushed tones.

The cashier rang Lucy up, eyeing her curiously. "Didn't your bakery provide cookies or something for the reading at the library yesterday?"

Lucy nodded, not wanting to discuss the event. It rubbed her the wrong way that the local establishments who had shunned Paula Peak in the past were now trying to profit by her death.

The cashier cracked her gum loudly. "Everyone's talking about that snobby author that died, but no one knows what happened. Do you know anything about it?"

Lucy shook her head, answering evasively, "I'm sure the police are doing a full investigation."

The cashier shrugged, bagging up Lucy's purchases and handing her the receipt.

As Lucy walked away, pushing her cart, she heard the cashier greet the customer behind her.

"Hey, Pam. You were at the library yesterday. Did you see what happened to that Paula Peak person?"

Lucy compressed her lips. *Small towns gossip*, she told herself. *That's just the way it is.*

The doors opened, and she pushed her cart through, heading for the parking lot. The establishment next to the grocery store was a pub called Jack's Lounge, and as she passed by, the door opened.

Stan Barclay stumbled out, almost crashing into her shopping cart.

"Oops… sorry," he tipped his hat as he straightened up. He offered an apologetic smile, but didn't seem to recognize Lucy.

She assessed his condition. While he didn't seem drunk, he wasn't sober either.

"Mr. Barclay," Lucy said. "It's me, Lucy Hale. I wanted to tell you… I am so sorry about… Ms. Peak." Her words were sincere. No matter how difficult or uppity the woman had been, Lucy was truly saddened by the tragic accident.

Stan squinted at her for a moment and finally seemed to place her.

COOKIE DOUGH AND BRUISED EGOS

"Yes. Ms. Hale, right?" He shook his head, his face showing his despair. "What a terrible thing. I still can't believe it myself. Paula was... she was so full of life. It's hard to believe she's really gone."

Lucy nodded sympathetically. "Were the two of you close?"

Stan sighed with a wry expression. "We'd been through a lot together. I'm the only agent she's ever had... I believed in her back when she was still writing her first book." His eyes looked faraway. "Back in those days, we had a lot of fun. She was a real lady, you know, classy dame." He chuckled slightly. "She'd knock me in the head if she heard me say that. But she was different back then." His eyes looked sad.

"Different how?" asked Lucy, genuinely curious.

Stan looked thoughtful. "Happier, I guess. Full of excitement about the future." His voice trailed off and Lucy thought he'd finished, but suddenly he frowned, shaking his head.

"Paula let success go to her head," he stated, seeming suddenly irritated. "She didn't know what she wanted anymore. She always thought she wasn't getting her fair share."

Lucy was confused. "Fair share?" she echoed. "Of what?"

Stan waved a hand. "Everything. She was dissatisfied with everything and everyone around her. Thought we were all holding her back. Even after everything I did for her, believing in her when no one else would, she was always cracking the whip. Lording it over me, threatening to replace me."

His face had darkened, and Lucy took a step back, surprised by how quickly his anger had popped up.

"*I* made her a star!" he proclaimed, pointing his finger at his own chest. "Without me, she would have been nothing."

Lucy edged away. "I should be going," she said, her hands tightening on the carriage handle. "I hope you have a safe trip home, Mr. Barclay."

He huffed out his irritation, saying curtly. "I won't be going anywhere anytime soon. Your deputy has instructed me to stay in town."

With that, he turned and walked away, and Lucy slowly exhaled.

Mr. Stan Barclay seemed to have a lot of pent-up resentment. She thought back to the argument she had witnessed in the library between Stan and Paula Peak.

Could that have been what it was about? Had Paula threatened to fire him?

Lucy loaded the groceries into her SUV, still a bit shaken by Mr. Barclay's ill temper. Even though he seemed very angry with Paula, Lucy still couldn't see how he could have murdered her. For one thing, he was standing right there with her and Hannah the whole time Paula was in the restroom. And secondly, you can't really make bees sting someone on command.

He was just a resentful man, and Paula's death was just an unfortunate accident, she told herself, backing out of the parking lot.

She tried to focus on something else, going over her plans for the cookie dough packaging and tallying the profit margin.

She found herself too distracted to crunch numbers, however, so after a few minutes she gave up, switching on the radio.

As she drove down the quiet downtown street, her local radio station cut into its musical program with a special announcement.

"…mysterious death of local celebrity, Paula Peak, author of award-winning novels, *Behind the Garden Gates* and *The Shadows Between Us*. According to an article in the Ivy Creek Ledger, the cause of death was found to be anaphylactic shock due to multiple bee stings. That's right, you heard correctly. Death by bee sting. What's more, an anonymous source has been quoted in the article, saying, according to the entomologist—that's a bug expert, folks—brought in by the Ivy Creek Police Department, the bees at the scene were found to be East African honeybees. In case some of you aren't up on your bee trivia, those bees are known by another name."

"Killer bees…" breathed Lucy, simultaneously with the radio announcer's shocking next words.

"Killer bees, right here in Ivy Creek."

11

*A*s soon as Lucy walked into the bakery, Aunt Tricia held up the newspaper.

"Have you seen this? The bees that killed Paula Peak were…"

Lucy nodded. "Killer bees. Yes, I just heard it on the radio. To be honest, I'm not sure what to make of it. It doesn't really change the fact that it was just an unfortunate accident."

Aunt Tricia looked through the windows apprehensively. "It's all anyone is talking about when they come in. I have to say, it's making me a little nervous. What if there's a whole swarm of them loose in town?"

Lucy set her packages on the counter. "From what I understand, they've been spotted in the U.S. before. I don't think the danger is like what you see in the movies. They're not out to hurt anyone."

Aunt Tricia raised her eyebrows. "Paula Peak might disagree."

Lucy sighed. "I ran into her manager. He's not taking the news well. He came out of Jack's Lounge ranting and raving about how he made her a star, and she never appreciated him. He also said Taylor asked him to stay in town."

Hannah came out from the back room just then.

"Lucy! Did you hear about..."

"The killer bees. Yes." Lucy nodded. "I need to go unload the flour at the back door. Can you help Tricia, Hannah? Looks like a group coming in."

The bell jangled and a posse of five women walked in, nervously chattering away. As Lucy headed for the back, the woman in front approached the counter, telling Tricia they'd be dining in, downstairs.

"We just heard there are killer bees in town. I think we'll play it safe and skip the veranda, even though the view is so pretty up there."

Oh, no, Lucy thought. *Are people going to start shying away from outdoor seating?*

She unloaded the SUV, glancing around at the side street. There were more than a few cars on the road, but foot traffic was lighter than usual. Word must be getting around.

As she walked back into the bakery, Hannah peeked her head around the corner.

"Taylor's on the phone for you."

Thinking she might get some answers from him, Lucy accepted the receiver gratefully.

"Hey, Taylor, what's up?"

"Why don't you tell me?" His familiar voice sounded distinctly cold.

Lucy frowned. "What are you talking about? I thought you were calling to give me a heads up about the bees…"

Taylor replied, "No, I'm calling to tell you to quit panicking the town. Do you know how many calls we've gotten with people frightened out of their wits, seeing killer bees on every corner? I'm trying to run an investigation. The fact that I'm now having to answer the phone every five minutes, trying to calm down residents, is making it very difficult."

Lucy bristled. "Me? Panicking the town? What are you talking about? I haven't told anyone about the bees at the scene."

Taylor pressed her. "No one? Not one soul?"

Lucy sighed impatiently. "Well, of course, I told Aunt Tricia. And Hannah, too. But neither of them went blabbing it to the town. And we didn't even know what kind of bees they were until it was published in the paper."

"East African honeybees, aka killer bees."

Lucy snapped, "Yes, I know that now! I'm telling you; it wasn't me who leaked the story."

Taylor was silent for a moment. "Well, then who? The only people outside my department who even knew there were bees found at the scene were you, Ms. Davidson, Mr. Farnsworth, and Mr. Barclay."

Lucy was done with his skeptical tone. "Here's an idea - why don't you call them all next and ask them. Or maybe just accuse them, since that's what you did with me."

She hung up the phone, mightily irritated with Taylor Baker.

Aunt Tricia peeked around the corner.

"We're swamped out here and running low on brownies."

"I'm on it," Lucy replied, tying on an apron.

The afternoon was busy, with the seating area inside staying almost full all day. The veranda, on the other hand, was noticeably empty. Lucy baked cookies and brownies non-stop, while Hannah helped Tricia out front. It seemed that as people chose to stay and eat their treats inside; they were tempted to buy more.

Or maybe it was anxiety eating, Lucy mused. Everyone was trading ideas on what little they knew about East African honeybees. Lucy decided she would do her own Google research when she got home.

Hannah finally appeared at her side. "OK, it's winding down out front. What should I jump on back here?"

Lucy consulted her list. "Muffins for the morning," she decided. "I'm going to whip up a few flavors of the cookie dough next."

Hannah grinned. "This might be great timing on the new cookie dough take-and-bake! I think many people will go for the idea, staying in, instead of venturing out."

Lucy smiled, thinking every cloud has a silver lining. "Well, they'll still have to venture out to pick up the dough!"

"Unless we start a delivery service..." Hannah remarked, with a sideways look.

"One thing at a time," Lucy chuckled.

They worked on separate projects in companionable silence for a while, and Lucy kept one ear tuned to the front, in case Aunt Tricia was overwhelmed by customers again. Her aunt was getting on in years, and Lucy wondered if she was taking on too much, running the front counter alone.

Heading out front with several containers of take-and-bake cookie dough, Lucy spotted a young woman approaching the bakery. She had long dark hair and appeared to be a few years younger than Hannah and Lucy.

She entered the bakery and smiled hello at Lucy.

"I have a question," she began, and Lucy held up her free hand.

"I don't have any news about the bees."

The woman laughed and shook her head. She seemed amused.

Lucy set down her packages, quickly arranging them in the refrigerated case beneath the new sign "Take-and-Bake Cookie Dough" and looked back at her.

"OK. What can I help you with?" Lucy asked. Aunt Tricia was upstairs taking a break in the office.

The woman offered Lucy an engaging smile and countered, "Well, I'm hoping I can help *you*."

She held out her hand, introducing herself. "My name is Betsy Henderson. I just moved to Ivy Creek, and I'm looking for a job doing counter help, preferably in a bakery."

Lucy raised her brows. She had just been thinking about hiring more help. *Ask, and you shall receive, indeed.*

She shook Betsy's hand. "Lucy Hale, the owner. Do you have any experience?" she asked, sizing up the woman. She had a firm handshake and maintained eye contact. She was polite and dressed neatly. *So far, so good.*

Betsy smiled and nodded. "Six years as a bakery manager in Hopewell, Indiana. My mother was a pastry chef, and I caught the bug—but I'm not a baker. My real talents are in organization and customer service. However, I do know my way around a kitchen… if you were ever in a pinch."

Lucy nodded approvingly. "Starting pay would be eleven dollars an hour." When Betsy nodded, Lucy continued. "I'll have to check your references, of course."

"Of course." Betsy retrieved a folded resumé from her purse and handed it over.

Lucy glanced down at the paper, then back at Betsy's face. "When would you be able to start?"

"Immediately."

Lucy chuckled. "How about tomorrow at eleven a.m.?"

Betsy grinned. "Sounds great."

After purchasing an iced caramel latte and a chocolate cupcake to go, Betsy took her leave, calling out, "See you in the morning!" The front door jangled, shutting behind her, just as Aunt Tricia came down the stairs.

"Who was that?" she asked, puzzled.

Lucy grinned. "That was your new assistant."

12

Lucy was exhausted when she got home that evening. She let herself in the front gate, too weary to even admire the flower gardens that her mother had established long ago.

Lucy had grown up in this house, and moved back in not long ago, deciding she'd feel better to have Aunt Tricia living with her, now that the woman was getting on in years. Before that, Lucy had made do with the apartment over the bakery, but this had proved a much better fit for her, as well as for her cat, Gigi.

She walked into the kitchen, yawning hugely. The events of the last few days, combined with her long hours at the bakery, were finally catching up to her. Aunt Tricia had left a note, saying she was having dinner with a friend. Lucy barely managed to put together a light supper for herself before her eyelids were drooping. She went to bed, falling asleep instantly, and woke up the next morning feeling quite refreshed.

And quite snubbed…. Gigi pointedly ignored her when Lucy entered the kitchen, the feline turning her back and twitching her tail as Lucy went about filling her dish.

"Aww, baby… are you mad at me for not spending any cuddle time with you?" Lucy cooed to her Persian cat, reaching down to stroke her fluffy white fur.

Gigi allowed herself to be petted but flattened her ears to show she was still miffed. After a minute she flounced away, curling up on the couch to fix Lucy with a baleful stare.

Lucy chuckled. "I see how it is. Maybe I'll have to bribe my way back into your good graces."

She decided to leave a little early and swing by Whiskers and Wags, the pet store in town. A new toy for Gigi might just do the trick.

The store was nearly deserted when she arrived, due to the early hour. Lucy roamed the cat aisles, browsing. It might be time to buy a new brush for her as well. Gigi loved being brushed and, with her long fur, it was necessary to keep on top of it.

The cat toy choices were staggering, filling both sides of an entire aisle. Lucy finally narrowed it down to two and became so engrossed in comparing a feathered wand toy to a battery powered mouse toy she didn't notice when a man came up behind her.

"Lucy." A familiar voice sounding near her ear caused her to jump.

It was Joseph, dressed more casually than she remembered ever seeing him. He wore jeans and a navy-blue golf shirt, and his smile flashed, warm and genuine.

"Hi, Joseph," Lucy put a hand to her chest with an embarrassed laugh. "You startled me."

"Oh, sorry," he apologized, then looked at the toys she held. "If you want my opinion, the wand is the better pick."

Lucy glanced down and then back up at him. "You have a cat?" She was surprised. For some reason, she would have pegged him as a dog person.

He held up two fingers. "Two. Siamese siblings, Yin and Yang. They are gracious enough to let me live in their house." He indicated the mouse toy. "That one didn't generate much interest, but the wand...hours of entertainment."

Lucy laughed, putting the mouse toy back. "That's exactly what I'm looking for. I'm on the outs with my cat, Gigi, since I've been so busy—she feels neglected, I guess."

Joseph nodded. "Exactly why I have two. They keep each other company."

He tilted his head. "Bakery doing well, then?"

Lucy grinned and nodded. "Yes, despite the bee scare in town. I actually had to hire more counter help yesterday."

Joseph waved his hand. "A lot of hubbub about the bees. It was tragic, to be sure, but unlikely that anyone else in town will fall victim to them. For one thing, they die after stinging, just like ordinary bees."

Lucy sighed. "It sure has generated a lot of anxiety, though. You didn't know Paula Peak, did you?" She was pretty sure Joseph was new to town.

He shook his head. "No, though I have read one of her books, *Behind the Garden Gates*, and I did find it intriguing. I may buy the new one, as well."

Lucy was surprised, and her face must have showed it, because he chuckled.

"Does it shock you that I read romantic suspense?" he teased, and her cheeks turned pink, a little embarrassed. He continued, "I had been planning to go to the event at the library, mostly because your bakery was providing the food. I had an important meeting come up, though, and couldn't make it."

Lucy was glad he didn't press her for the details surrounding the tragedy, as others had. She nodded and smiled, then changed the subject. "How's the theater business going? Is your summer schedule set yet?"

Joseph smiled. "Not yet—but it's coming along. I think we're going to have a tremendous season."

He looked at his watch. "I actually need to get over there. I just stopped in to pick up this." He held up a package of treats. "The only treats the twins will deign to eat."

Lucy laughed. "And I thought my Gigi was spoiled."

Joseph grinned. "Oh, I'm sure she is." He tilted his head to one side, looking at Lucy inquiringly. "Say, there's a new Greek restaurant in Colby, just a short drive away. I've been wanting to try it. Would you like to go out to dinner sometime?"

Lucy hesitated. She really liked Joseph's personality, but she wasn't sure how she felt about him romantically. She stalled.

"Greek, really? That's different from what we usually see around here."

Joseph nodded, his eyes gleaming. "I've been hankering for some spanakopita. My grandmother made the best. That and her baklava..."

Lucy smiled. "I've never made baklava. It looks complicated. But it is delicious."

"It's a little time-consuming," Joseph admitted, "But I'm sure you could master it. And it's so worth it. I actually have her recipe, if you'd like to give it a try?"

Lucy grinned. "I love trying new recipes! Yes, please. Next time you're in the neighborhood..."

Joseph nodded, "Sure. I've been meaning to swing by the bakery anyway for some apple turnovers. I can drop off the recipe later. And think about dinner, will you, Lucy?"

He turned away, looking back to give her a small wave, and off he went.

Lucy stared down at the feathered cat toy in her hand, her thoughts a jumble. Joseph was a really nice man. They got along well; they had a love of cats in common...

Why was it she found herself so reluctant to start dating again?

13

When Lucy got to the bakery, things were already hopping. She stepped in to help Aunt Tricia with the morning rush, thinking it was great timing that Betsy would start training today. By the time Hannah arrived, the crowd had dissipated, with a few small groups even opting to sit on the veranda upstairs. Thankfully, the panic over the bees seemed to have subsided somewhat.

"We've already sold five packages of cookie dough," Lucy informed Hannah, who grinned and high-fived Lucy.

"Guess I better get started then." Hannah tied on an apron, disappearing into the back while Lucy and Tricia headed to a table to sit for a moment.

"So... your new assistant should be here shortly," Lucy commented, eyeing the clock.

Aunt Tricia sipped her iced mocha. "Well, I'd be lying if I said I didn't need help out here," she said with a sigh. She looked up at Lucy, concern on her face. "Are you sure we can afford it?"

Lucy nodded without hesitation. "Absolutely. Sales are really picking up, and I see no reason to believe they won't continue to increase."

She changed the subject. "Guess who I bumped into this morning at Whiskers and Wags?"

"Oh, so that's where you were. Spoiling that cat again..." Aunt Tricia teased. "I give up. Who?"

"Joseph Hiller from the theater. It turns out he has two cats of his own. Even more spoiled than Gigi, I'd say." Lucy grinned.

"Hard to believe," Aunt Tricia commented, and Lucy chuckled.

"Well, anyway, we got to talking, and he told me about his grandmother's baklava... said he'd let me use her recipe. What do you think? Would it fly?"

"Only one way to find out."

Lucy nodded. "Might as well give it a shot. He told me there's a new Greek restaurant opening up in Colby, so there might be a local interest."

Aunt Tricia looked at her speculatively. "A new Greek restaurant, huh? And how did that come up?" Her eyes gleamed with interest over her tortoiseshell glasses.

Lucy shrugged. "He asked me to dinner. I didn't really give him an answer because I'm not sure how I feel about him. I mean, he's a very nice man..."

Aunt Tricia patted Lucy's hand. "Again... only one way to find out. Take a chance, dear! It's time you moved on from Richard."

COOKIE DOUGH AND BRUISED EGOS

Lucy sighed. "It's not really about Richard. We weren't that serious—that whole relationship seemed more about convenience. Honestly, Auntie, I haven't really lost my heart to anyone since... before I moved to the city..." She let the thought go, remembering how annoyed she was with Taylor right now.

Just then, the bell jangled as Betsy walked in, and their conversation was cut short. *Right on time*, thought Lucy, *on multiple levels.*

The next few hours passed in a blur, with Lucy training Betsy on the POS system and answering her questions about their products. She was very impressed with Betsy's attentiveness—the woman had even brought a small notebook in which to jot things down.

Lucy was just instructing Betsy on the use of the cappuccino machine when the bell jangled again. She looked up to see Joseph entering the bakery.

"Hi," she greeted him, coming over to the counter. Seeing the paper he held, she added, "Is that your grandmother's baklava recipe?"

"It is." He handed it over with a flourish and then looked at Betsy with a polite smile.

Lucy introduced them and couldn't help but notice how Betsy's eyes lingered on Joseph's face, her cheeks turning pink. She seemed instantly smitten. Lucy hid her smile and scanned the recipe, noting the ingredients. *They'd need to get more honey, but she had everything else in stock.*

"Looks perfect!" She indicated the display case. "Joseph, didn't you say you were wanting some apple turnovers? Please accept a half dozen on the house, as a thank you."

Joseph grinned. "Great! Thanks, Lucy."

Betsy murmured, "I'll bag them up for you." With a shy smile at Joseph, she moved away.

Lucy nodded approvingly, watching Betsy slip on gloves, then came out from behind the counter, joining Joseph at the new display of Take-and-Bake cookie dough.

"Wow, great idea," he commented, looking at Lucy admiringly. "So, Lucy…have you given any thought to my dinner invitation?"

Lucy hesitated, then decided the best thing to do was be straight. "Thank you, Joseph, but I'm not looking to start dating right now." She looked into his handsome face with an earnest expression. "I do enjoy your company. I hope we can continue our friendship."

Joseph smiled, his green eyes crinkling. "Of course. Maybe we can still get together sometime—as friends only. In the meantime, feel free to call me if you need a baklava taste-tester."

Lucy laughed and nodded; glad his feelings weren't hurt. "I certainly will. I value your expertise in Greek pastries."

They chatted for a minute more, then Joseph said he had to be going. He accepted his package from Betsy and turned to leave, telling the young woman he was pleased to have met her.

As he opened the door to leave, he nearly collided with Taylor, who was coming in. Joseph apologized, stepping back and allowing Taylor to come inside first.

Stepping into the doorway, Joseph looked back over at Lucy. "Just say when!" He waved at the ladies and exited the store.

Taylor turned to watch Joseph walk down the sidewalk with a peculiar look on his face, then turned to face Lucy. She raised her brows and folded her arms, wondering what he wanted. Taylor looked inquiringly at Betsy.

Crisply, she made introductions. "Taylor, this is Betsy. She'll be helping at the counter. Betsy, this is Taylor Baker, the deputy sheriff."

Taylor nodded and smiled genially at the girl, then met Lucy's eyes. "May I please have a word with you in private?"

His tone was conciliatory, which mollified Lucy enough to agree. Calling Hannah in to help Betsy until Aunt Tricia returned, Lucy led Taylor upstairs to the office.

They had no sooner settled into their chairs when Taylor began.

"First off, I want to say I'm sorry for jumping to conclusions. I found out who leaked the story—it was one of my officer's wives. I never should have assumed it was you, Lucy. Please accept my apology." He seemed very sincere, his blue eyes staring into hers.

Lucy nodded. "OK. I accept your apology. I hope you realize though; I would never breach your trust. We're friends, Taylor, and I understand your day-to-day job involves very sensitive information. I wish you trusted me enough to realize you can tell me things and they'll be kept private." She amended her statement, seeing the look on his face. "Well... private, as in, I might tell Aunt Tricia, because I tell her everything."

Taylor chuckled. "Yes, I know that about you." He sighed, leaning back and rubbing a hand over his sandy hair. "I've got to tell you, Lucy, this case is getting to me."

"Not going well?" Lucy sympathized.

Taylor shook his head. "I'm positive this was no accident, and I'm pretty sure Geoff Farnsworth was involved. It turns out he had a serious motive for wanting his wife dead."

"Life insurance?" Lucy took a stab in the dark.

He nodded. "And he was the only person that we know of that left the room to follow her. I just can't figure out how he did it." He sighed and rubbed his eyes. "I can't ask him to stay in town forever."

Lucy was silent, envisioning the scene as she remembered it. She wished she'd had time to look around more closely—she might have seen something that would be helpful. But she'd been too involved in comforting Geoff.

Taylor stood. "I need to get back to the station. I just wanted to make sure everything was OK between us."

Lucy stood as well, offering a smile. "Of course, it is. Let's get you fixed up with a coffee and raspberry Danish to go. They just came out of the oven."

She led the way down the stairs, only half-hearing Taylor as he commented on the weather forecast. An idea had taken root in her mind and wouldn't let go.

She was determined to have another look at the crime scene.

14

Throughout the next morning, Lucy was distracted by her idea to have another look at the library restroom. *Maybe she'd be able to spot something that would help Taylor in his investigation.*

After the lunchtime rush, the pace slowed down a bit, and Lucy decided to take advantage of the lull.

"I'm going to go out and see what I can find for more honey," she announced. "If we start making baklava, we'll have to buy it in bulk, and I'm not sure if Bing's sells it that way."

"You really should look into buying local honey," Betsy piped up. "If you eat local honey, it helps with seasonal allergies. That might be an additional selling point."

Lucy nodded, liking the idea. "Good thinking. I'll look and see what's out there." She took off her apron and hung it up. "I'll be back in an hour or so."

As soon as she got into her hot car, she wished she'd brought a cold drink with her. *Maybe she'd stop in at the café,* she mused. She didn't want Richard to think there were any hard feelings about their breakup, and it had been at least a month since she'd stopped in.

Traffic was light, and Lucy arrived at the café in minutes. The cool rush of air conditioning that greeted her when she opened the doors made her sigh in relief. It wasn't usually so hot here this early in the year, but they seemed to be having a warm spring.

As she moved to stand in line at the counter, she noticed a familiar figure seated at a small table in the middle of the shop.

Stan Barclay. His ever-present fedora was pushed back from his forehead, and he was hunched over, talking on his phone with a worried expression. He seemed to be upset about something, drumming his fingers nervously on the tabletop, and clutching the phone tightly.

"Next, please."

Lucy looked up and realized she was next in line. A young woman she'd never seen before was behind the counter, smiling patiently. Lucy placed her order and scanned the back area while the woman made her iced latte. Richard was nowhere to be seen.

She paid for her coffee and turned away, but her curiosity got the better of her. She decided to detour by Stan's table. As she approached, she heard him say, "I told you - I'll have the money tomorrow!"

He hung up the phone and wiped his forehead with his sleeve, looking dejected. Lucy's gaze landed on a folded newspaper on the table. The horse racing section was face up, and she spied several picks circled in red.

Lucy froze, unsure if she should just turn and go, but it was too late. He'd spotted her. He stared at her with his brows raised questioningly, looking annoyed at the intrusion.

"I... ah, hello... is everything alright?" she stammered, not sure of what to say. She wished now she had left straight away.

Stan frowned at her. "Just peachy." He eyed her suspiciously. "Is there something I can do for you, Ms. Hale?"

Lucy tried to think of something to say to explain her approach but came up blank. She shook her head and turned away, feeling Stan's eyes on her as she left the coffee shop. She got into her car and turned on the air conditioning, cooling her flushed cheeks.

Well, that was awkward.

She wondered who he'd been arguing with... he'd sounded defensive. *A bookie?*

Lucy pondered how that might possibly play into Paula Peak's tragic death but couldn't come up with a plausible connection. Obviously, Stan owed someone money but, surely, he couldn't profit from his client's death. *Could he?*

Lucy shook her head, dispelling the unanswered questions, and put the car in reverse. It was time to take another look at the crime scene.

She pulled into the library parking lot, noting a red hatchback was the only car there. Perfect! That must be Clara's car, and she'd have the librarian to herself as she did her snooping.

Lucy exited her car, iced coffee in hand, and walked up the stone steps. She grasped the handle of the heavy oak door and gave it a pull, but it didn't budge. She rattled it back and forth, thinking maybe it was stuck, but no.

It was locked. *Odd.*

There was no sign on the door, indicating that Ms. Davidson had needed to step out. Lucy peered through the glass, trying to see inside. The lights were on. *How peculiar.*

She rapped smartly on the door and waited. A minute passed and she knocked harder, but there was still no answer. Lucy looked through the glass again but couldn't see any activity inside.

Stumped, she turned and slowly descended the stairs, heading for her car. *Well, that was a bust. How strange for the library to be closed in the middle of the day, with the lights on, and no "Closed" sign.*

As she reached her car, Lucy peered at the shady lot surrounding the building. Perhaps there was a back door she could knock on? She approached the side of the building and saw a small window set up high. The screen was torn. That was the old restroom window…

Walking into the shadows provided by the maple trees, Lucy headed around back. The asphalt here was cracked and weeds straggled upward, reaching for a way out of the gloom. Lucy spied a blue dumpster set behind the library and eyed it speculatively. *Had anyone checked the restroom trash for clues?*

She looked down at her black and pink bakery chef jacket and grimaced. She was not exactly dressed for dumpster diving and knew it would be unwise in broad daylight, anyway. But she could always come back at night… That is, provided it didn't have a lock on it.

COOKIE DOUGH AND BRUISED EGOS

She scanned the front and didn't see one. Ducking her head under a cobwebbed branch, she walked around to check on the back.

A figure suddenly popped up from behind the dumpster, startling her, and Lucy stumbled backwards, stifling a shriek.

It was Geoff Farnsworth.

15

He regarded Lucy with a scowl as she pressed a hand to her chest, feeling her heart stuttering.

"Mr. Farnsworth," she gave a shaky laugh. "You scared me to death!" She looked around the lot curiously, not seeing a second car. *Maybe it was his red hatchback out front?*

"What are you doing here?" she asked, puzzled.

He strode toward her, and Lucy backed up a step, nervously.

"I could ask you the same thing," he commented. He raised his eyebrows.

Lucy's thoughts whirled. *If the library was closed, why would Geoff Farnsworth be hanging around? Was he intending to break in? For what purpose? To hide evidence?*

Her suspicions must have shown on her face because he suddenly looked impatient, snapping, "I didn't kill her, you know. If the police in this town would stop wasting time, trying to pin her death on me, maybe they'd actually find out what happened! I came here myself, looking for answers, but the library seems to be closed."

He looked at her defensively, hands on his hips, but Lucy wasn't sure what to say. He seemed awfully angry, and she was becoming more uncomfortable by the moment. Way back here, almost behind the building, they couldn't be seen by anyone passing by.

She shivered, the hairs on her arms standing up.

Geoff huffed out a breath and suddenly brushed past her. Lucy watched him walk out of the shady back lot, her pulse slowly returning to normal. She observed him, wondering if he would head to the front parking area, but he took a left onto the side street instead, and within minutes, he was out of sight.

She gave another speculative look at the dumpster, deciding she would come back tonight and see if she could find any clues.

After all, Geoff had been crouched down behind there for some reason. She wasn't entirely convinced by his story of trying to exonerate himself.

She pondered the events of the day. Between Stan's hostility and evident gambling habit, and Geoff's suspicious behavior, she was starting to believe that foul play may well have been involved in the death of Paula Peak. But still, the questions swirled through her mind.

Could Stan somehow profit enough from the author's death to pay off his apparent gambling debts? How? And if it was Geoff behind the murder... if indeed it was murder, how exactly did he pull it off?

Lucy looked uneasily in the direction Mr. Farnsworth had gone. If he was a murderer, and thought she suspected him...

A cold chill ran down her spine. She decided she'd better play it safe and confide her suspicions about both men to Taylor.

After all, that's what the police were there for, right?

A SHORT DRIVE LATER, Lucy was pulling into the parking lot of the Ivy Creek Police Department. As soon as she opened the door, she could hear the hum of activity. Several phones were ringing, and a middle-aged man with glasses was sitting at one of the officer's desks, complaining loudly about his neighbor's late-night activities.

The dispatcher, Fran, winked at Lucy as she came in. She was on the phone at the front desk, speaking in a soothing voice.

"Well, I'm sure the bees at your hummingbird feeder are just ordinary bees, Mrs. Green. No need to worry." She jerked a thumb in the direction of Taylor's office, nodding to Lucy that she was OK to go right in.

Lucy rounded the desk just as the bespectacled man said insistently, "But I know he's violating the noise ordinance…"

She rapped lightly on the glass of Taylor's half-open door, and heard him say, "Come in."

As she entered the office, she saw he was perched on the edge of his desk, talking on the phone. He held up a finger, nodding at a straight-back chair. Lucy eased herself into it, gathering her thoughts.

"Yes. Yes, I understand. No, I don't think we'll need you to appear in court, but we will need documentation of your findings. Thank you for your time. Goodbye."

He hung up the phone and sighed, rounding his desk to sit behind it.

"Hey, Lucy. What brings you in here?" Taylor's face looked weary, his hair standing on end as though he'd ran his fingers through it. Lucy had a sudden, surprising urge to smooth it and kept her hands fisted tightly in her lap.

She leaned forward, hoping he would take her concerns seriously.

"I've had two strange encounters today, Taylor, and I thought I should let you know."

His eyebrows raised. "Oh? With whom?"

Lucy met his eyes. "One with Stan Barclay, and one with Geoff Farnsworth."

Taylor frowned, waiting for her to continue.

Lucy filled him in on the conversation she'd overheard at the café first, mentioning the newspaper with gambling picks circled in red. She watched Taylor's face with a sinking feeling as he began to look impatient, tapping his fingers on the desk. She hurried on to describe her encounter with Mr. Farnsworth but, halfway through it, he interrupted her.

"Why were you at the library?"

Lucy flushed. "I was… I wanted to thank Ms. Davidson for hiring Sweet Delights."

Taylor looked skeptical. "In person?"

Lucy nodded. "But the library was closed. Actually, that's kind of odd, don't you think?"

Taylor waved away her concerns. "Maybe she had to go out."

"But her car was there," Lucy said, then hurried on. "Mr. Farnsworth was in the back parking lot, behind the dumpster. Don't you think that's a little suspicious?"

Taylor pinned her with a look. "And why were you in the back parking lot, if the library was closed?"

Lucy shook her head, frustrated. "Why does *that* matter? I'm not a suspect in the murder."

Taylor pointed a finger at her. "Correct. And neither are you a law enforcement officer. So, if you have it in your head to poke around for clues, I want you to forget about it right now, Lucy. I mean it. Leave the investigating to me."

Lucy huffed out a breath. "Can't you see I'm only trying to help?"

Taylor stood up. "I've got work to do, Lucy."

He walked her to the office door. "Say hi to your Aunt Tricia for me. I didn't see her when I was at the bakery yesterday. By the way, who was the man that was leaving when I came in? I know I've met him before but can't remember where."

Lucy stared at him, confused by his abrupt change of subject. "Joseph? The theater director?"

Taylor's eyes narrowed. "Oh, yes. I thought I heard him say, "Just say when", when he left. Are you dating him now?"

Lucy's temper flared. "That's really none of your concern, Taylor." She turned away. "Go ahead, get back to your work. Don't let me stop you."

Head held high, she walked out of the police station, fuming. It stung that Taylor had been so blatantly dismissive of her speculation.

That made her even more determined to uncover the evidence that he had missed.

16

The next morning, as Lucy was cutting the test batch of baklava into diamond shapes, Betsy appeared at her elbow.

"I've never made baklava. Was it difficult?"

Lucy shook her head. "Kind of tedious maybe, coating each sheet of phyllo dough with melted butter, but not hard to make. You do have to keep an eye on the honey syrup, though, because it will scorch easily."

She noticed Betsy's intense regard for the pastry. "If you like, you can help me with the next batch."

Betsy grinned. "I'd love that! I really want to master some Greek cooking...especially Greek desserts." She bit her lip, looking around, and then confided. "I'd like to get to know Joseph better. Do you know if he's dating anyone?"

Lucy smiled at the young woman. "Actually, I happen to know that he's not."

Betsy nodded, pleased. "Maybe I could make some baklava myself, to bring to him at the theater." Her hazel eyes twinkled as she regarded Lucy. "My mom always said the way to a man's heart is through his stomach."

Lucy laughed. "Now, there's a saying that has some truth to it!"

Just then, Hannah came in through the back door, calling out, "Good morning!"

The screen door slammed behind her. Hannah hung her purse on a hook and walked into the kitchen, tying on her apron. She spotted Lucy cutting the pastry.

"Baklava!" she crowed, looking at it admiringly. "Looks great, Lucy. Are you going to call in Joseph Hiller to taste-test it?"

Lucy laughed. "Although he *will* be one of the taste-testers, I thought we'd all try it first. Even though I'm using his grandmother's recipe, I do want to put my spin on it, so I made a few small changes."

"When do we get to try it?" Hannah asked eagerly, while Betsy looked at Lucy hopefully.

"Hmm..." Lucy grinned at them. "Now? Baklava for breakfast, anyone?"

Aunt Tricia popped her head around the corner from where she'd been manning the front counter. "Did I hear that we're sampling the baklava? I'll go get some napkins. No customers right now—perfect timing!"

Hannah spied the recipe laying on the metal workbench and picked it up, scanning it.

"Wow, takes a lot of honey." She glanced up at Lucy, who was busy serving up the small diamond-shaped pastries. "Did you have any luck finding a bulk supplier?"

Lucy shook her head and passed Hannah her piece as Aunt Tricia reappeared with a handful of napkins. "No. I stopped at Bing's as well as that market on the edge of town—Newland's Grocery—but neither carried anything larger than a 20-ounce jar."

"Mmm..." Betsy nibbled at her pastry. "I could get used to this."

Aunt Tricia murmured her agreement, eyes closed as she sampled the new product.

"Don't change a thing," Hannah stated after swallowing a bite. "It's perfect."

Lucy was a little more critical, and took her time concentrating on the melding of flavors. "I think it's just a touch too sweet," she announced. She set down her napkin, jotting a note into her recipe book. "But if we bump up the vanilla..."

The bell jangled and Aunt Tricia and Betsy both set down their napkins, heading for the front to greet the customers.

"I think this will be super popular," Hannah declared. "We need to figure out a honey source pretty quickly."

Lucy nodded. "I'll do some research on it at home. Maybe there's a bee farm in the nearby mountains."

"That's a great idea! Speaking of bees, what's the buzz around town?"

Lucy groaned, fixing Hannah with a look.

Hannah smirked. "Sorry, couldn't help myself. But seriously is everyone still talking about the bees? And has Taylor told you anything about the progress of the investigation?"

Lucy's brows beetled. "I think the town's still pretty panicked. I stopped by the police station, and you could tell they're still getting tons of calls from worried citizens—everyone thinks the killer bees are in their own backyard."

Hannah helped herself to another piece of baklava, picking at the flaky crust. "Why were you at the police station?"

Lucy sighed, remembering her frustration with Taylor. "I had two very strange encounters yesterday, one with Paula's husband and one with her manager. They both were acting very strangely." She quickly filled Hannah in on the details.

Hannah looked surprised. "The library was closed in the middle of the day? That's odd."

Lucy nodded. "And stranger still - I think Ms. Davidson was there. Does she drive a red hatchback?"

Hannah nodded. "She sure does." She took another bite and chewed slowly, pondering. "What do you think Mr. Farnsworth was doing lurking in the back parking lot?"

"He claimed he was looking for clues, so he can prove his innocence," Lucy answered dryly. "Although, his very presence there made me suspect he may be guilty after all. I think it's possible he was trying to cover his tracks... maybe destroy evidence he left behind."

She looked at Hannah speculatively. "He was behind the dumpster. Maybe he had the same idea as I did—to find the trash from the restroom that day. Maybe there's something in there that he's afraid will lead the police back to him... *if* he's the killer," she amended.

COOKIE DOUGH AND BRUISED EGOS

Hannah considered Lucy's words. "Don't you think the police would have bagged up the trash as evidence already?"

Lucy shrugged. "Possibly. But remember - at first, they were pretty convinced it was an accident. The bathroom trash could have been tossed out with the rest during the clean-up after the event."

Hannah's eyes gleamed. "Only one way to find out!"

Lucy regarded her friend hopefully. "Does that mean you're volunteering to go with me tonight? I figured after dark, no one can see the library's back parking lot from the street. And I didn't see a lock on the dumpster."

Hannah stood up, brushing crumbs off the table. She threw her napkin into the trash and turned back to Lucy with a grin.

"*You* can do the dumpster diving, but I'll be your look-out."

Lucy high-fived her. "Deal."

17

It was only just after 9 p.m., but the streets of Ivy Creek were practically deserted. *One perk of living in a small town*, Lucy thought, as she and Hannah crept quietly into the library's back parking lot. The blue metal dumpster gleamed in the moonlight, and Lucy looked around apprehensively. What would she say if someone caught them?

Hannah must have seen her glance around. "No one can see us back here," she reassured Lucy. "And besides, I'll keep watch. I'll let you know if someone's coming."

Lucy nodded, swallowing nervously. Although this had seemed like a fine plan in the light of day, now she was having second thoughts. She steeled her nerves, approaching the dumpster. The only way to get through it was to do it!

She pulled on a pair of yellow latex gloves and lifted the lid slowly, wincing as the metal hinges creaked. Carefully, she opened it all the way, until the lid settled against the back with barely a thud. Peering inside, she was grateful that the contents didn't stink to high heaven. *Well, it was a library, after all, not a seafood restaurant.*

Glancing once at Hannah, who was vigilantly watching the street, Lucy lifted herself up on the edge, balancing on her belly, and reached inside. There appeared to only be three large, black trash bags. *Good. That would make it easier!*

One by one, she lifted out each bag, depositing them on the cracked pavement behind the dumpster. She debated against closing the lid before she opened the bags, but decided it would be safer if she did. In the event someone happened by, an open dumpster may attract attention. The hinges creaked again as she closed the lid, setting it down with minimal noise.

"OK," she whispered to Hannah, who turned and joined her, crouching in the deep shadows behind the dumpster.

They each had a flashlight, and switched them on, the twin beams illuminating the dark plastic bags. Without further ado, Hannah slipped on her own pair of gloves and untied the bag nearest her. Lucy looked at the two remaining bags and chose the fullest one.

Within minutes, Hannah looked up. "Party trash," she whispered, and tied it back up.

Lucy had just discovered the same with her own bag. Just dirty paper plates, plastic utensils, and a lot of used napkins. She tied hers back up, too, and reached for the last bag. Hannah peeked over the top of the dumpster, then squatted back down, shining her light on the bag while Lucy untied it.

Bingo! The large black bag contained two smaller white bags —trash from the restrooms. Lucy and Hannah simultaneously

COOKIE DOUGH AND BRUISED EGOS

untied the bags, opening the tops wide enough to peer inside. Hannah held the flashlight while Lucy pawed through a pile of crumpled paper towels, finding nothing unusual in the first bag. She retied the red flaps and moved onto the second one.

Spreading the bag wide open, she noticed something strange right away. There was an almost full sheaf of pristine paper towels, folded and stacked as they came from the factory, ready to be loaded into a dispenser.

"That's weird," she mumbled, frowning. She thought back to the scene, with Paula Peak lying on the floor. She was positive there were several crumpled paper towels scattered around the woman, as though she'd only just finished drying her hands when she was stung.

Lucy moved the stack out of the way to look further into the bag. She was mystified at what she found next.

Banana bread. A lot of it.

She glanced up at Hannah, whose puzzled expression mirrored her own. There looked to be an entire loaf of sliced banana bread in the trash, though the pieces were broken and tumbled together.

That didn't make sense. This was obviously the restroom trash - the bags were much smaller. Why would someone have tossed an entire loaf of banana bread into the bathroom trash receptacle?

She checked through the rest of the bag, but there was nothing else. Unused paper towels and banana bread were all it contained. Not even any used paper towels. The ones on the floor must have been collected as evidence.

Suddenly, a car door shut nearby. It sounded like it was across the street. Hannah switched off her flashlight immediately. Heart pounding, Lucy hastily tied up the bags in the dark, and then they both waited. Listening.

There was silence for a minute, and then another door shut, a quieter thud. Lucy relaxed. *It was only someone coming home to one of the houses across the street.* Hannah stood, slowly peering over the top of the dumpster. She looked down at Lucy and flashed an OK sign with finger and thumb.

"Coast is clear. I'll stand watch," she said, dropping her gloves onto the ground next to the trash.

Within minutes, Lucy had quietly deposited the bags back inside the dumpster, adding both pairs of latex gloves. She closed the lid, and she and Hannah scooted quickly out of the parking lot, heading for Lucy's SUV, parked down the street.

Once they were inside, Lucy turned to Hannah, voicing her questions.

"What do you think that was all about? Banana bread in the restroom?"

Hannah shook her head. "Almost a whole loaf? I have no idea. Even if it had been dropped and had to be thrown out, why the restroom trash?"

Lucy reached for her keys and suddenly noticed her phone was blinking, indicating a voicemail. She held up a finger to Hannah as she listened.

It was Taylor. He sounded concerned.

"Lucy. I think you should be aware; Geoff Farnsworth appears to have skipped town. We have a BOLO out for him, but given your recent interaction with him, I thought you should be warned. Keep an eye out and please keep your doors locked. If he thinks you suspect him, he might come after you. Call me when you can."

Shocked, Lucy down set the phone, looking at Hannah with wide eyes.

"Paula Peak's husband skipped town. I think we've found our murderer."

18

Lucy tossed and turned in bed all night, unable to stop thinking about the case. She had called Taylor when she got home, but he didn't have anything additional to tell her. Just repeating that Geoff Farnsworth had checked out of his hotel, disregarding Taylor's instructions that he stay in town. The police were looking for him, and Taylor wanted Lucy to remain vigilant.

Lucy finally gave up on sleep, tying on a robe and wandering out to the kitchen to make some tea. Gigi greeted her, winding around Lucy's legs, purring, pleased that her favorite human was awake. Lucy gave her a treat and settled down in front of her computer, sipping her tea. If she was going to be up, maybe she could do some research.

She typed in "East African Honeybees" and spent the next fifteen minutes browsing articles. As she had mentioned to Aunt Tricia, this wasn't the first time they had been spotted in the United States. Although there was a ban on importing them, it was suspected that they were a black-market commodity, the same as many exotic animals. Lucy yawned, finishing her tea, and powered down her laptop. She hadn't learned anything of value to the case, except that if someone really wanted to obtain killer bees, with the right connections and a lot of money, they could probably do so.

Geoff Farnsworth had money, she mused. *And he had run, which made him look guilty. But how did he pull it off?* She was determined to get a look inside the library restroom and see if there was anything she'd missed.

She left a note on the table for Aunt Tricia, explaining that she'd had a sleepless night, and would be coming into the bakery late. With the additional help of Betsy, she was sure the ladies could handle the morning rush without her.

With Gigi padding lightly at her heels, Lucy went back to bed.

AT TEN O'CLOCK THE next morning, Lucy was pulling in next to Clara Davidson's red hatchback in the library parking lot. She cast a glance toward the dumpster in the back lot, relieved to see it looked undisturbed in the light of day.

She walked through the doors and spotted Clara shelving books near the left front wall.

"Good morning, Clara," she greeted the woman, who looked surprised to see her.

"Hello, Lucy," Clara answered. "What brings you here?" She removed her spectacles, letting them dangle on the chain she wore. She appeared a bit fatigued, the lines on her face even more prominent than Lucy remembered.

"Oh, just driving by, and I thought I'd see how you were..." Lucy answered, waving her hand. "I imagine it was no easy thing to return to work, after all that happened."

Clara compressed her lips and nodded. "It was a bit difficult," she admitted. She looked around the empty library. "And it seems to have had its impact on the readership of the town, I'm afraid."

Lucy nodded sympathetically. "I'm sure it was... but the town will bounce back, you'll see."

Clara tilted her head. "Would you like some coffee? I was just about to have a cup."

Lucy smiled. "That would be great. Thanks."

Clara led the way into the small office, and switched on the Keurig machine, gesturing to a leather chair opposite the desk. "Please, have a seat. It will just be a moment."

While it brewed, Clara thanked Lucy again for catering the event, adding that she planned to come into the bakery soon to place a pie order. Moments later, she was seated behind the desk, and both ladies sipped at their coffee.

"Did you hear about Mr. Farnsworth?" Clara asked her, and Lucy raised her brows, surprised that Clara knew. The woman continued, "The police called me this morning, telling me they suspect he murdered Paula. Apparently, he left town, and they're trying to track him down now."

Lucy feigned ignorance. "But how could it have been murder? She died of shock from the bee stings."

Clara frowned. "I couldn't imagine. But somehow that man did it. I bet he stands to inherit all of her money." Her voice had a bit of an edge to it.

"I'm sure the police will find him," Lucy commented. She set down her cup. "Clara, if you don't mind, I'd like to use the restroom." She stood up. To her dismay, Clara stood as well.

"Of course," the woman answered. She walked to the office doorway with Lucy, pointing to the public restroom door across the hall. "It's right there."

Lucy was stumped. She'd hope to just scoot out and use the private restroom down the hall, but how could she do that with Clara watching her?

"Thanks," she said, crossing the hall and entering the bathroom. She stared at her own reflection in the mirror, wondering what to do. With a flash of inspiration, she turned on the tap in the sink and filled her cupped palms. She threw the water on the floor, hoping the sound of the fan covered any noise. A few handfuls more and she quickly dried her hands, leaving the room. Only a minute had passed since she had first opened the door.

Clara was still standing at the office doorway. She looked surprised to see Lucy exiting the bathroom.

"I hate to tell you, but it looks like that toilet is broken, Clara!" Lucy fibbed. "There's water all over the floor like the seal is leaking." She turned into the long hallway, calling over her shoulder, "I'll just use the private restroom."

She walked quickly away, feeling the librarian's eyes on her back. She reached the door marked *'Employees Only'* without incident, however, and wrenched it open with a loud screeching noise. Shutting the door behind herself, she leaned her back against it, heart beating fast.

She looked around the small room. Her skin prickled as she remembered Paula Peak's lifeless body on the cold white tiles. Her gaze drifted up, to the screen, still ripped, flapping lightly in the breeze.

Moving across the room, she stood beneath it, inspecting it closer. The edges were not jagged, but clean, as though something had sliced through it.

It was cut, not torn.

The realization sent a chill through her. *Had the murderer cut the screen, trying to make it look like the bees had come in that way?*

She peered into the trash next, but the bag was empty. Turning slowly, scanning the room, she didn't see anything else unusual. She flushed the toilet, washed her hands at the sink, and then reached for a paper towel.

The dispenser was empty. Lucy frowned, remembering the stack of factory-new paper towels in the trash. She dried her hands on her jeans, not knowing what to make of it all.

With a few hard pulls and a lot of noise, she managed to get the heavy, wooden door back open, and stepped into the hallway.

Clara was standing there, waiting, and Lucy jumped guiltily.

The woman offered a smile that didn't reach her eyes. "Just making sure you didn't get stuck," she said lightly, then turned her back and led them down the hall.

"Oh, thanks," Lucy said. "By the way, your paper towel dispenser is empty."

Clara stopped. She turned to Lucy with a frown, her gaze suspicious.

Lucy was a bit taken aback by the woman's expression. "Just thought you should know…"

Clara nodded curtly and continued down the hall to the office. "I believe you left your purse in there, Lucy."

The librarian's demeanor had definitely taken a chilly turn. Lucy retrieved her purse and thanked Clara for the coffee. They walked to the lobby together, and Lucy had the impression she was being shown the way out.

She turned to Clara, hesitantly asking, "Ah… is everything OK?"

Clara raised her eyebrows. "Apparently not." Her tone was clipped. "It appears I need to call a plumber."

With that, the woman turned, walking back into the library, while Lucy stepped out into the sunshine, welcoming the warmth on her skin.

She couldn't shake the feeling that she was missing something important—a piece of the puzzle, right in front of her, but still hidden.

19

"And I'll take five packages of the chocolate-chip dough, please," Mrs. Gibb requested, opening her wallet. "My youngest is having a sleep-over birthday party, and I think the girls baking their own cookies would be the perfect theme!"

Lucy grinned, overhearing this as she made a caramel latte for another customer. The cookie dough sales were exploding. She was already thinking of adding another flavor to the selection. *Maybe we should do a flavor of the month*, she mused.

She heard the back door shut and glanced at the clock, pleased that Hannah was early. Finishing up the coffee order, she hurried into the back to let Hannah know what they were running low on.

"I'm so glad you're early, Hannah. We're going to need chocolate-chip dough right away. Mrs. Gibb just about wiped us out. And we're down to three apple turnovers. I'll come back here to help as soon as Betsy returns."

"Returns from where?" Hannah asked curiously, washing her hands.

Lucy grinned. "Well, instead of having Joseph come here to taste-test our baklava, I sent Betsy over there with some samples."

Hannah chuckled. "Oh... playing Cupid, are we?" She, too, must have noticed Betsy's interest in the theater's production manager.

Lucy gave her a sly smile. "I do what I can," she said modestly, and Hannah hooted with laughter, tying on her apron.

Lucy returned to the front, assisting Aunt Tricia, and the morning flew by. They were so busy she barely had time to ponder yesterday's visit to the library. It wasn't until Taylor walked through the door, his expression grim, that her thoughts turned once again to the murder.

Thankfully, the morning rush was about over. Taylor made pleasant chit-chat with Aunt Tricia until the last customer left the store, then turned serious, his eyes on Lucy.

"I have some news about Geoff Farnsworth."

Lucy gripped the counter, and she felt Aunt Tricia move closer. In her peripheral vision, she caught a glimpse of Hannah hovering at the doorway, having heard Taylor's voice.

"Have you caught him?" Aunt Tricia voiced the thought that was in all of their minds.

Taylor nodded, and a breath whooshed out of Lucy. She hadn't realized how worried she'd been until that very moment. She could still picture Geoff's angry face in her mind, as she'd last seen him behind the dumpster.

"Yes," Taylor said. "He was apprehended in Montana, and they're holding him for us. Of course, he's still protesting his innocence, but there's little doubt in my mind that he's guilty." Taylor ticked the points off on his fingers. "He had the most to gain from Ms. Peak's death. He knew she didn't have her EpiPen on her. And he skipped town. Circumstantial evidence, of course, but in this case, it's all we have to work with. He'll be formally charged with her murder in the next few days."

"Thank goodness," murmured Aunt Tricia.

"What about the bees?" inquired Hannah. "Have you figured out how he pulled it off?"

Taylor held up a hand. "We're still investigating. I can't discuss the details. I just wanted to let you know," he nodded to Lucy. "You don't have to worry about Mr. Farnsworth coming after you."

Lucy nodded, absorbing the information. Her thoughts swirled in her head. She wondered if she should mention the things she'd discovered to Taylor. The screen being cut, not ripped; the strange contents of the restroom trash...

She looked at his handsome face, remembering his words. *I mean it, Lucy. Leave the investigating to me.*

She decided to leave well enough alone. Maybe now that Mr. Farnsworth was in custody, all the pieces of the puzzle would start to come together.

"Thank you for stopping by, Taylor," she said. "Would you like an apple turnover? They just came out of the oven."

His eyes lit up, and Lucy packed one up for him. A few minutes later, he said his goodbyes, heading back out.

As soon as the front door closed behind him, Betsy came in through the back. She was beaming as she joined the ladies out front.

"Joseph said the baklava is delicious, Lucy! He wants to place an order as soon as it becomes available to the public. He said it's just as tasty as his grandmother's, even though he could tell it was slightly different." Betsy's cheeks were pink and there was a definite sparkle in her eyes.

Lucy smiled at her, raising an eyebrow. "You seem pretty happy. A good visit to the theater, then?"

Betsy laughed, blushing further as she confessed. "Joseph asked me to dinner. I'm so excited! We'll be trying that new Greek restaurant in Colby on Friday."

Aunt Tricia squeezed her shoulder. "That's fantastic, Betsy. You two make a cute couple."

Lucy and Hannah agreed, and Betsy looked pleased. She looked around at the cases.

"Wow, busy morning?"

Hannah nodded. "I could barely keep up! Now that you're here, though, Lucy and I can stock us back up together."

Lucy glanced at the clock. "Aunt Tricia, you've been on your feet all morning. Why don't you take a break?"

The woman sighed, untying her apron. "Sounds like a plan. I'll be up on the veranda if you need me, Betsy." She snagged herself a muffin and headed for the stairs.

Hannah and Lucy went into the back and got to work. An hour and a half later, they had managed to get all caught up, and Lucy's thoughts turned to their new product: baklava. She crunched some numbers in her head. At the price they were paying for honey in small containers from Bing's Grocery, it would be hard to make a profit. She really needed to find a supplier to buy the honey in bulk.

She grabbed a sandwich and iced coffee and headed upstairs to her office. Settling down at her desk, she booted up her laptop, and initiated a search for bee farms in the area. The point that Betsy had made, that consuming local honey was proven to help with seasonal allergies, had stuck in her head. It would be a good marketing angle, and she liked the idea of supporting local small businesses.

Several bee farms popped up in the nearby mountains, and Lucy clicked on their websites, scanning through them. One in particular appealed to her.

Bee Natural, a honeybee farm that sold raw honey in quantities as large as a gallon, was only two and a half hours away. They had some interesting products for sale, as well, including honey candy, soaps, lotions, and beeswax candles. *It might be nice to offer some of their products on the front counter, too,* she mused.

She hit the button to print out the directions. Tomorrow morning she'd take a trip out there with Hannah—they'd stocked up well enough today to get them through till the afternoon.

At the back of her mind was an idea she refused to fully acknowledge.

Could the beekeeper at Bee Natural shed some light on the murder of Paula Peak? Specifically, how someone could orchestrate a bee attack?

20

"Aw, gee..." Hannah's voice on the telephone sounded disappointed. "I would love to go, but Mrs. Warner called yesterday. She needs her dessert tray a day early."

Lucy reassured her. "Oh, it's fine, Hannah. I just thought it would be fun, but I'll go by myself this time. You can come with me next time. I'm sure we'll need more honey in a month, if the baklava catches on."

She chatted with Hannah for a minute more, sharing her idea of possibly carrying assorted products from Bee Natural at Sweet Delights, and Hannah took to the idea immediately. Their conversation concluded, and Lucy disconnected the speakerphone, focusing on the road ahead.

The drive up to Swansboro was a pretty one, cutting through picturesque valleys and following meandering rivers. Lucy was caught up in admiring the view, barely noting the passing of time. Printing out the directions had proved to be a sound decision, as only halfway into the trip, her phone signal wavered and then disappeared completely, taking the GPS with it. The route was pretty straightforward though, and she found the town of Swansboro without any trouble. As she entered the little mountain community, she noticed a hand painted sign, pointing the way to Bee Natural Honeybee Farm.

Five minutes later, her tires were crunching up a steep gravel road, set high above the valley. An enclosed farm stand came into sight, with a sprawling white farmhouse set well behind it. In the field beyond, Lucy spotted rows upon rows of crates lined up, which she assumed were the hives.

She had called first thing this morning and chatted with Nina Ford, the beekeeper and sole proprietor. As soon as she parked her SUV, a tall, lean woman dressed in coveralls came out of the farm stand, waving a hand.

"Lucy?" the woman called, with a welcoming smile. "Hello, I'm Nina."

Lucy joined the woman, shaking her hand. "It's a pleasure to meet you."

Nina led them inside, and Lucy looked around the small building in awe. Tables were filled with baskets of peaches and containers of strawberries, and jars of honey lined the front counter. There was an entire wall devoted to bee products such as candles, soaps, and lotions, and wrapped candy sticks in assorted flavors stood in a jar labeled "Bee Sweet".

"Wow, all of this came from your farm?" Lucy asked, amazed. She turned and looked at Nina with growing respect. "Does your family help out?"

COOKIE DOUGH AND BRUISED EGOS

Nina laughed, a pretty, tinkling sound and nodded. "When I can corral them, I have three teenage boys! No, seriously, everyone lends a hand, especially in the spring."

She followed Lucy's gaze to the counter full of honey jars. "Oh, that's the standard size I sell, but I do have gallon jugs available."

"Oh, good!" Lucy was pleased. "I think I'll start with just one gallon, but I'd like to sell some of your products in the bakery, as well."

Nina was delighted, and the next ten minutes were spent with Nina explaining a little about each product and the production process. The woman was a font of information, and Lucy wished she were able to take some notes. She looked at Nina hopefully.

"You wouldn't happen to have brochures, would you?"

Nina grinned and reached down behind the counter, coming up with a handful of Bee Natural flyers. "How about these?"

"Perfect!" Lucy said, tucking them into her purse. She scanned the array of products, choosing a few of each item, and Nina tallied her order, adding one gallon of honey.

Their business concluded. Nina walked her out to her vehicle, and Lucy packed her purchases away.

"Do you have time for a tour?" Nina asked. "I have an extra suit for protection, if you'd like to see the hives."

Lucy shook her head regretfully. "I've got to get back, but maybe next time." She looked out over the valley, admiring the magnificent view.

"Gosh, I bet you never get tired of seeing that!" She regarded Nina quizzically. "Do you ever feel isolated all the way up here? Cut off from the town?"

Nina chuckled. "Never! I couldn't care less about what's happening in the rest of the world. I don't watch the news or read the newspapers. I have my own little paradise right here. Why spoil it?"

Lucy hesitated, not wanting to bring up the killer bee attack, but still itching for answers. "You know, I've always been curious about bees. There's more than one kind of honeybee, right?"

When Nina nodded, Lucy pressed forward. "Are some of them more dangerous than others? Like... more likely to sting you?"

Nina considered her question. "All bees will sting to protect their hive, or their queen. But as far as aggressive? Well, there's the East African honeybee, which is known to be more aggressive. As far as honeybees that are native to this area, if they don't feel threatened, they'll pretty much leave you alone."

"East African honeybee... those are the ones they call killer bees, right?"

Nina cocked her head, suddenly seeming puzzled. She nodded slowly. "Yes, but they're banned from being imported into the US. If they're found on container ships coming into port, the bees are destroyed."

Unless they're sold on the black market, Lucy added silently. Nina was looking at her quizzically, so Lucy decided to wrap it up. She did have one last question, though.

"Is there anything, besides perceiving a threat to the hive, which will make bees more aggressive?"

Nina frowned, and Lucy wondered what she was thinking. She seemed to be considering the question carefully. She finally answered, looking Lucy in the eye.

"Certain soundwaves, like high-pitched noise. They don't like that. And some scents that mimic the pheromone released by panicked bees. Bananas is a good example. If bees detect a banana scent in the air, they react by being aggressive, because that's what agitated bees smell like, to other bees, at least."

Bananas... For a moment, Lucy drew a blank, knowing that was significant, but not remembering why. Then, suddenly, the image of the banana bread in the trash flashed in her memory, and she gasped.

It had been placed there deliberately to antagonize the bees!

"Lucy? Are you OK?" Nina was peering at her in concern, having heard Lucy's sharp intake of breath.

Lucy covered by glancing at her watch. "I just noticed the time, that's all. I need to get back to the bakery. Thank you so much, Nina! I'm sure I'll be back soon." She started edging toward the door of her car, her mind whirling.

Nina smiled graciously. "It's been a pleasure doing business with you, Lucy. Do you have a business card for your bakery handy?"

Lucy nodded. "Oh, yes, of course." She pulled the pink and black Sweet Delights card out of her purse, handing it over with a smile. "You'll have to stop in sometime, Nina... if you ever decide to come to Ivy Creek."

Nina looked surprised. "Ivy Creek! That's so strange." Her green eyes met Lucy's.

"You're the second person to visit from Ivy Creek in the last month, asking questions about bee behavior."

Lucy's mouth went dry, and she could hear her heartbeat thudding in her ears.

"Who was the first person? Did you get a name?"

21

Nina scrunched up her face, trying to remember. "I don't recall her name. A middle-aged woman... reddish hair, glasses... drove a red hatchback."

Lucy turned white as a sheet, gripping her car door. "Clara Davidson?"

Nina tilted her head, thinking. "Could be. I can't quite remember. She asked almost the same questions as you. What makes bees aggressive, that sort of thing. It was for some sort of project... what was it?" She held up her hand. "Oh, I remember, now."

"She said she was an author, researching for a book about killer bees."

Lucy's mind went numb with shock as the realization dawned.

Clara was the killer! She had cut the screen and filled the trash can with banana bread... she knew Paula wouldn't use the public restroom...

Her thoughts racing, she barely managed to say goodbye to Nina. Gripping the steering wheel tightly, she backed down the driveway and turned onto the mountain road, trying to understand.

Clara... because she'd never forgiven Paula for stealing her story. But how did Clara contain the bees in the restroom? And how did she know Paula wouldn't have an EpiPen on her person?

With shaking hands, Lucy reached for her phone. *She had to tell Taylor! They were planning to charge Geoff with Paula's murder.*

A sudden curve took her by surprise, and Lucy hastily applied her brakes, swerving to stay on the pavement. Her heart raced at the close call. She needed to find a place to pull off. The road was too treacherous, with a steep drop off on one side.

With every minute that passed while she navigated the winding lane, Lucy felt her urgency increase. She remembered how strange Clara had acted after she had used the private restroom. *Did Clara suspect she was on to her?*

Finally, the road widened, and Lucy was able to pull off to the side. She picked up her phone, but noticed the signal only showed one bar. With a sinking feeling she dialed the Ivy Creek Police department, but, just as she'd feared, the call was dropped after one ring. *She had to get off this mountain before she'd have a good enough signal.*

Her knuckles were white as she gripped the steering wheel, going as fast as she could manage safely. She found herself wishing for a speed trap—if she happened on a cruiser, they'd be able to contact the Ivy Creek Police for her. But the road was sparsely traveled, and Lucy continued on, glancing down at her phone's display every few minutes.

COOKIE DOUGH AND BRUISED EGOS

Finally, as she entered a valley, the signal bars jumped up to three, and Lucy abruptly pulled to the shoulder, dialing the number with trembling fingers. She crossed her fingers Taylor or Fran would answer, but instead she heard an unfamiliar voice.

"Ivy Creek Police Department. Officer Frye speaking."

Lucy cleared her throat. "Yes, hello, may I speak to Deputy Baker, please? This is Lucy Hale." She clutched the phone tightly, her mouth dry.

"Sorry, Deputy Baker is out of the office. May I help you with something?"

Drat. Lucy closed her eyes, concentrating on the right way to convey her information.

"Um, yes. This has to do with Paula Peak's murder. I've just found out some information about... well, I think I know who killed her, because..."

The officer interrupted her. "Rest assured, ma'am. We have a suspect in custody."

Lucy interjected, "But you have the wrong person! Geoff Farnsworth isn't responsible! It's really..."

"Ma'am, like I said, we have a suspect in custody. It will be up to the courts to decide from here on out."

With a click, the line went dead. Lucy stared down at her phone incredulously.

He hadn't listened to a word she'd said! She was tempted to call right back, but she knew it wouldn't do any good. Instead, she dialed Taylor's cell phone next.

It went right to voicemail, which meant it was either switched off or he was on a call. Knowing how Taylor preferred to communicate with his officers through his radio, she assumed his phone was switched off. Still, maybe he'd see he had a new voicemail.

The beep sounded in her ear, and she rushed into her message.

"Taylor, it's Lucy. I was just up at a bee farm in the mountains, and the beekeeper said Clara Davidson was here a month ago, asking questions about bees... and aggressive bee behavior... and the screen in the library restroom was cut, Taylor, not ripped! I think Clara..."

The beep sounded again, ending the recording, and Lucy gritted her teeth in frustration. She tossed her phone on the seat and pulled back onto the road.

She tried Taylor's cell several more times over the next hour along the route home, hoping he'd pick up. The phone would ring once and just go to voice mail, but now she was getting a recording saying the voice mailbox was full. Lucy drummed her fingers on the steering wheel impatiently, thinking.

She'd go straight to the Ivy Creek Police Department. She now regretted never telling Taylor the story that Clara had relayed to her—how Paula Peak had stolen her idea for a book and turned it into a best-seller. It was a motive for murder, and she'd never recognized it as such. But she'd tell him now, as well as all the other details she'd foolishly kept to herself. If Clara was indeed the killer, and she thought Lucy was on to her, she might be planning to run. For all Lucy knew, Clara could have already left town.

It was that thought that had her suddenly turning off of Main Street as she entered Ivy Creek an hour later. She decided to loop around Gardner Road and pass by the library on her way to the police station. If she didn't see Clara's red hatchback, she could tell Taylor the librarian might have already skipped town. They could put out a BOLO right away.

Lucy slowed down as she approached the library, her eyes scanning the nearly empty parking lot. Clara's red hatchback was there, alright, and there was only one other car parked near the entrance.

Her blood froze in her veins as she recognized the blue sedan.

It was Aunt Tricia's car.

22

Lucy spun the wheel sharply, turning into the library parking lot. Aunt Tricia rarely drove these days – it couldn't be a coincidence that she was at the library when she was supposed to be at the bakery!

Lucy jumped out of her car and ran to the library's front door. It was locked. There were no lights on inside.

Her heart in her throat, she frantically pounded on the door with her fists.

"Clara! Aunt Tricia!" She banged again, then peered through the glass. She didn't see anyone inside. Her pulse raced. She'd never forgive herself if something happened to Aunt Tricia!

She pounded on the door again, but hearing nothing, jogged around to the back parking lot. It was deserted. Lucy eyed the small bathroom window with the cut screen. If she could only find a way up there...

She needed something to stand on. She spied an old five-gallon bucket on the ground near the dumpster - that might be tall enough. As she approached the heavily shadowed area, she thought she heard a noise behind her. She whirled around, but no one was there.

The isolation of the back lot filled her with unease, and she decided to give Taylor one more try on his cell. If she didn't reach him, she'd call the police department next, and then she'd try to get in that window. There was no time to waste. Aunt Tricia could be in danger! She dialed Taylor's number, and it rang once, twice, three times, before he picked up.

"Taylor!" she cried, relieved beyond measure that he'd finally answered.

Something suddenly struck her arm from behind, numbing it, and the phone dropped from her grasp, clattering on the pavement. She whirled around just in time to see a dark cloth descending upon her face.

Lucy struggled, shrinking back from the chemical fumes as the rag was pressed firmly over her nose and mouth. Within seconds, everything went black.

———

HER HEAD ACHED TERRIBLY, and her mouth tasted foul. Lucy slowly drifted back into consciousness, becoming aware of her surroundings a little at a time. She blinked in the gloom, trying to understand what had happened. *She'd been in the back parking lot of the library...*

All at once, everything came rushing back, and her body went rigid.

Clara was the murderer!

'Aunt Tricia!" Lucy's cry was muffled, and she realized there was a gag tied tightly around her head. She kicked her legs and tried to move her arms, panicked to find herself bound, hand and foot.

In the darkness, she heard an answering mumble, in a voice as muffled as her own. She squinted in the dim light, her eyes slowly turning shadows into objects. There was a furnace, and some yard maintenance tools... a grimy window set up high. A staircase.

She must be in the library's basement. She heard another moan and swiveled her head, finally locating the source. A figure was sitting propped up crookedly against the far wall, and Lucy's heart leapt into her throat as she recognized her aunt. She appeared to be bound and gagged as well. Lucy strained her eyes, anxiously trying to see if Aunt Tricia was injured, but the shadows obscured her, and there was no way to tell.

Lucy flexed her arms, wiggling her wrists, and found a little play in the rope that bound her. If she could just get loose before Clara returned...

She concentrated, ignoring the pain that traveled up her arms, trying to fold her thumb into her palm to slip past the binding. As she grimly worked at the rope, she tried to come up with a plan. The window, set at ground level, was too high to escape from. The basement was underground but there must be a bulkhead door. Probably located on the wall across from the staircase. The shadows were too deep for her to tell for sure... and what if it were locked?

Lucy cast her eyes about the dim cellar, looking for a weapon. The leaf blower on the pallet was probably her best option. If she could get free, she could hide behind the staircase and surprise Clara when she returned.

What if she never returned?

The chilling thought hit Lucy all at once. What if Clara had already left town? Would anyone think to look in the basement of the library? She tried to remember if she'd told Officer Frye who she thought the killer was. She was pretty sure he had hung up on her before she said Clara's name.

But Taylor would know! Lucy sagged with relief, remembering. She had left him a voicemail about Clara. He would see her car, and Aunt Tricia's sedan in the parking lot, and she was sure he would search the building thoroughly, including the basement. Clara might be on the run by then, but at least she and Aunt Tricia wouldn't die, hidden away in this cellar.

They just had to hang on until Taylor got here. Lucy heard Aunt Tricia moan again, and her heart plummeted.

What if Aunt Tricia was hurt? How much time did they have?

Lucy doubled her efforts, wincing as her hand was rubbed raw, but she still couldn't get loose. *There had to be a way!*

A door suddenly creaked above her, and Lucy froze, hearing it open.

She'd run out of time.

Lucy's gaze fixed on the staircase; her mind filled with dread. Footsteps were heard slowly descending the steps before the figure came into view.

A slim panel of light spilled from the open door at the top of the stairs, slicing into the gloom of the cellar. It illuminated Clara Davidson as she deliberately paused, fixing Lucy with a malevolent smile.

"Oh, good, you're awake," she commented conversationally, sliding her right forearm down the banister as she slowly descended the last few steps.

Light flashed on the object clutched in her fist as she approached, and Lucy's blood ran cold.

In Clara's hand was a large butcher's knife, the blade gleaming wickedly.

23

Lucy swallowed; her eyes fixed on the knife. She was more afraid than she'd ever been in her life. Clara walked slowly toward her, gesturing with the knife as she spoke.

"Well, Lucy, you've saved me a phone call. I was going to have to lure you here with your aunt as a hostage, but instead, you came to me! How very convenient." As Clara spoke, she idly caressed the blade with one finger, and Lucy held back a shudder.

Clara's face was twisted into a sneer, her hair disheveled. In her eyes was the bright, fanatic light of madness. Lucy heard a soft moan from Aunt Tricia but stopped herself from glancing her way. The last thing she wanted was for Clara to focus her attention on her aunt.

Lucy wriggled and mumbled to distract Clara, and the librarian studied her, head tilted inquisitively.

"I have to say, I'm not sure how you figured it all out. You must be smarter than you look. Smarter than this town's bumbling police force!" She scoffed. "What a joke."

A small, satisfied smile appeared on her face. "Did you hear that the police have apprehended Geoff Farnsworth? As soon as they figure out you and your aunt have disappeared, I'm sure they'll be charging him with three murders, not one. The husband is always the first suspect, you know. I was betting on that."

She shook her head with mock regret. "It's too bad you were so nosy, Lucy. As soon as you contrived that little scene with the water on the floor so you could use the private restroom, I had my suspicions. And your face when you came out - I knew you were on to me, then. Snooping around…very bad manners, Lucy." She tapped the blade of the knife with her fingernail. "Very bad, indeed."

She sighed, and her eyes looked dreamy. "I will say, you've inspired me to write again! You and your suggestion to use life's painful experiences for a new novel." She laughed, and the tinkling, joyful sound echoed, eerily out of place in the gloomy cellar.

Lucy shivered, the hair rising on the back of her neck as Clara leaned over her. "I'm going to turn this all into a best-seller, Lucy. Too bad you won't be around to read it. This will all be first-hand experience, how it feels to kill and get away with it. First, Paula, then you… and then your lovely Aunt Tricia."

Lucy's eyes widened in horror, and Clara looked amused. She looked at Lucy with an inquiring expression. "Did you ever figure out how I got the bees into the restroom? I'd hate for you to die with unanswered questions. And besides, it was so very clever... I think you'll appreciate the ingenuity."

Lucy shook her head, trying to keep Clara talking. *If she could just buy some more time, she knew Taylor would figure out where she was.*

Clara looked delighted. "Ha! I knew you hadn't figured out everything! The bees—which cost me dearly, I'll have you know—were contained in one of those little cardboard envelopes. Now, this was the tricky part... I certainly didn't want to be stung accidentally. So, I emptied the paper towel dispenser, leaving just a few sheets at the bottom, snipped a tiny corner of the envelope, dropped it in, and closed the top." She grinned, the madness back in her eyes.

"Voila! I imagine those bees were pretty stirred up, trapped in that metal dispenser. Just waiting," Clara sneered, "for our *lovely* author to come and free them when she dried her hands! Paula had always been so vain. I knew she wouldn't carry an EpiPen on her person."

Her expression turned rueful. "Of course, I didn't think about *afterwards*. Since I didn't know if all the bees had come out of the dispenser. I couldn't risk filling it back up with paper towels."

Clara's tirade had slowed, and Lucy frantically tried to think of a way to stall her. She bobbed her head up and down, mumbling into her gag insistently.

"What? What's this nonsense?" Clara eyed her. "If you scream, I'll kill your aunt in front of you... slowly."

Lucy bobbed her head, and Clara reached down and pulled the gag from her mouth.

Lucy gasped for a breath, free of the foul-smelling rag.

"You should... just go..." she croaked out. "Run, before it's too late. You don't need to kill us."

Clara shook her head. "No, I don't need to. But since I've already killed, I might as well try a new method. For the experience..." She reached down as if to pull Lucy's gag back up.

Suddenly, a thud could be heard from upstairs. Both Lucy and Clara looked up, sharply.

Lucy's heart hammered in her chest as she prayed. *Let it be Taylor.*

She looked at Clara, the librarian's face twitching nervously as she clenched the knife in her hand. *This could still end badly if Clara thought the cops were here.*

"It's Hannah," Lucy bluffed. "I called her from the parking lot. She must have come in the front door."

Another thud from upstairs. Lucy held her breath.

"The front door is locked," Clara said, swiveling her head to eye Lucy suspiciously.

Lucy insisted. "I know it's her. She's probably seen our cars by now."

Clara hesitated, and Lucy willed the woman to believe her. If Clara thought she was cornered, who knew what she'd do?

Clara yanked Lucy's gag back over her mouth, then crept quietly up the stairs to look.

As soon as the librarian was out of sight, Lucy heard the creak of a window. She spun her head to see Taylor's head and one shoulder filling the small basement window. He was lying on the ground outside, and his gun arm was extended into the cellar, pointing at the staircase.

Lucy caught his eye, then looked over at Aunt Tricia, hoping he would understand.

All at once, the booming sound of the front door being kicked in upstairs reached her. The library echoed with shouts.

"Police!"

"Clara Davidson! Put your hands up!"

Footfalls pounded on the stairs, and Lucy shrank back in horror, as she saw Clara come running down, with the knife pointed right at her!

"You!" the woman shrieked at Lucy, who flinched, squeezing her eyes tightly shut, thinking this was the end.

Taylor's voice boomed out. "Freeze!"

Lucy peeked through her eyelids. Clara had stopped on the last step and was regarding Taylor in the window, with a calculating look in her eyes.

"Drop the knife, or I'll shoot," he commanded in a steely voice.

Just then, the sound of many boots pounding through the library could be heard, and there was a commotion on the stairs behind the librarian. Wide-eyed, adrenaline coursing through her veins, Lucy witnessed Clara being arrested and handcuffed, the knife clattering down to the floor.

Several more officers thundered down the stairs, and Lucy watched gratefully as they reached Aunt Tricia, bending to minister to her first.

A weak cough was heard, and then her aunt said, "I'm OK."

Lucy's body sagged with relief, trembling with shock from their close call.

It was over.

24

"I still can't believe it," Hannah said, shaking her head. "Clara Davidson... she's been the librarian for ages. She went to school with my mom."

She finished cutting the peach pie, serving Taylor a slice first. She, Lucy, Tricia, and Taylor were seated at their favorite table in the bakery. It was several days after Lucy and Tricia's harrowing experience, but Lucy's mind was still reeling from all that had happened. Thankfully, neither she nor Aunt Tricia had sustained any injuries, although Taylor had insisted they both be checked out at the hospital. Aunt Tricia had explained to Lucy in the ambulance that Clara had tricked her into coming to the library, calling to say Lucy had dropped in to have another look at the restroom and suddenly taken ill.

"It's a good thing you thought to leave me that voicemail, Lucy," Taylor commented. He forked up a piece of pie as Hannah finished passing out slices. "Without it, Clara might have gotten away with it. As it stands, she's looking at fifteen years in prison, minimum."

"One thing I don't understand, Taylor, is why Mr. Farnsworth skipped town?" asked Aunt Tricia, puzzled. "He was innocent."

Taylor shrugged. "I guess he was afraid to take his chances in court. He looked guilty, with that large life insurance policy he had on his wife."

Lucy nodded, remembering what Clara said. *The husband is always the first suspect.* "And Stan Barclay… he was acting so suspiciously, but I guess he was just a gambler on a losing streak."

Taylor harrumphed. "Just as well, Mr. Barclay left town yesterday. He said he was returning to the West Coast. They can keep him."

Hannah sat down and turned to Taylor. "Have you found out where Ms. Davidson got the bees?"

Taylor looked grim. "All she would tell us was, in her extensive research, she's discovered that anyone can buy anything they want, if they spend enough money."

He shook his head. "I hate to say it, but she's right. There's a huge black market operating throughout the United States—most people aren't even aware of it."

Lucy picked at her pie, still coming to terms with it all. Clara Davidson had come up with a dark, but brilliant way to rid herself of her enemy, and make it look like natural causes. The woman was highly intelligent, but her mind was twisted. Lucy shuddered to think of what might have befallen her and Aunt Tricia if Clara hadn't been stopped.

The bell jangled, and Betsy walked in with Joseph, laughing and chatting. Taylor straightened up, observing the happy couple with surprise. He glanced sideways at Lucy.

The pair approached the table, and Betsy turned serious, asking Lucy and Tricia how they were feeling.

Lucy could feel Taylor's eyes on her as she answered.

"Grateful," she said, meeting Taylor's familiar blue gaze. She glanced up at Betsy with a smile. "I'm feeling grateful... and safe, and none the worse for wear."

Taylor reached across the table and gave her hand a squeeze, while Betsy engaged Aunt Tricia in conversation.

"Lucy," he said, his voice too low for the others to hear. "You gave me a scare."

Lucy looked at him, remembering all the times he'd been there for her... through thick and thin. She smiled warmly at him, pushing his plate closer.

"Eat your pie, silly man," she teased him, pulling her hand away. He grinned and picked up his fork again, and she watched him fondly, the adage ringing in her head.

The way to a man's heart is through his stomach.

The End

AFTERWORD

Thank you for reading Cookie Dough and Bruised Egos. I really hope you enjoyed reading it as much as I had writing it!

If you have a minute, please consider leaving a review on Amazon or the retailer where you got it.

Many thanks in advance for your support!

A STICKY TOFFEE CATASTROPHE

CHAPTER 1 SNEAK PEEK

CHAPTER 1 SNEAK PEEK

Lucy taped the brightly colored flyer to the bakery's front counter, where all the customers would see it. Betsy looked over her shoulder, her face wreathed in smiles.

"This is going to be so much fun!" she exclaimed, her hazel eyes alight with excitement. "I can't wait to pick out a costume!"

Lucy grinned, excited, herself. Ivy Creek was having their first annual Fairy Tale Fair, and Sweet Delights Bakery would be a vendor. All vendors were required to be in costume, and she suspected a lot of the townspeople attending would be dressing up, too.

It was exactly what Ivy Creek needed to get past the scandalous murder that had happened only months ago. Lucy suppressed a shudder, thinking of the close call she and Aunt Tricia had been subject to at the hands of Clara Davidson, the town's librarian turned murderess.

Hannah came through the kitchen door, bearing a tray of freshly baked muffins. She arranged the pastries in the display case before joining them to check out the flyer.

"So, what theme will we have for our booth?" she asked curiously. She knew Lucy had hired a few of the college kids who worked at the theater to custom design their bakery stand.

"A Gingerbread House," Betsy announced, then glanced at Lucy sheepishly. "Joseph told me." Betsy had just recently started dating Joseph Hiller, the theater's production manager.

"Oh, how cool is that?" Hannah exclaimed. "Will we dress up as Hansel and Gretel, a witch, and a woodcutter?"

Lucy shook her head. "I thought of that, but when I went to the costume shop in town, they'd sold out of Hansel and Gretel. I think we should all just pick something we like. I'm considering going as Cinderella—I've always liked that fairy tale best."

Aunt Tricia, who had been setting up the cappuccino machine, looked over her shoulder with a sly smile. "I think you should! And Taylor should go as Prince Charming."

Taylor was the town's deputy sheriff, and an old flame of Lucy's. When Lucy had moved back from the city upon the tragic death of her parents, Taylor had been quite cool to her, resentful, she supposed, that she'd left her hometown behind. But as time went by, and she showed her commitment to stay and run her parent's bakery, he'd warmed to her considerably. Now they were fast friends again, and Lucy had felt the simmering attraction between them growing stronger.

"I think Taylor has his own costume planned," she told Aunt Tricia. "He said it's a surprise." Aunt Tricia raised her eyebrows, but refrained from further comment, much to Lucy's relief.

Lucy was glad Aunt Tricia approved of Taylor, but she needed to be careful she wasn't jumping into anything too fast. The last thing she needed was any awkwardness between herself and her old flame. Taylor was just too important in her life for her to lose his friendship again.

"How about you, Aunt Tricia?" Lucy asked. "Didn't you go to the costume shop this morning?"

Her aunt smiled smugly. "I did. And I snagged the only Ice Queen costume they had left. I tell you, girls, you'd better rent your costumes soon. I know for a fact they've sold out of all their princess costumes. Gina told me she'd had a dozen in stock, anticipating a run on them, but they went like hotcakes."

"Oh, no." Betsy looked worried. "I better get over there tonight with Joseph."

Lucy glanced at the clock. Ten minutes until they opened. She grabbed her notebook and pen and picked up her coffee, heading for her favorite table by the window. Customarily, the small staff had a pow-wow right before opening on Wednesday mornings.

Hannah and Aunt Tricia joined her, splitting a muffin and settling into their chairs. Betsy, ever industrious, grabbed a rag and Windex to work on the storefront window next to them while she listened.

"OK, guys..." Lucy tapped the pen on the pad. "I'm thinking we should use the opportunity of the fair to launch a new product. Any ideas?"

Hannah mused out loud. "Well, if you're planning to have samples at the fair, it has to be something that can stand the heat."

Aunt Tricia sipped her coffee. "I've always thought we should start a line of candies, but chocolate wouldn't do well outside all day."

"Candy would be a nice change... doesn't have to be chocolate," Lucy murmured, thinking.

Betsy piped up, scrubbing at a spot. "How about toffee? It's temperature stable." She turned to face Lucy, rag in hand. "And you could also crush it to use in your other products, like brownies or cookies."

Lucy smiled. "That's a great idea!" She scribbled on the pad. "We can make different varieties, too."

They spoke for a few minutes of what pastries were likely to sell best at the fair before Aunt Tricia looked at the clock. She stood and pushed her chair back in. "Show's about to start, ladies."

She and Betsy rounded the front counter, straightening the displays, as Hannah disappeared into the back room to continue the day's baking. Lucy unlocked the door, and flipped the sign to "Open", then sat back down, crunching numbers and making notes.

The bell rang just minutes later, and Mrs. White, one of their best customers, breezed in with a cheery "hello".

A STICKY TOFFEE CATASTROPHE

She stepped up to the front counter and eyed the display, pointing immediately to the key lime tartlets. "Oooh… that is just what I'm looking for! Can I have six of those, please?"

As Betsy boxed up her order, Mrs. White noticed the flyer. "Will Sweet Delights be at the Fairy Tale Fair, then?" Anticipation sparkled in her eyes, magnified behind tortoiseshell glasses.

Aunt Tricia smiled, ringing her up. "Yes, we will! Just look for the gingerbread house booth."

Mrs. White chuckled. "Oh, my, that's perfect. How ingenious!" She accepted her receipt and packaged tarts, grinning as she proclaimed, "This is going to be the event of the summer. See you all there!"

She gave Lucy a little wave as she passed through the front door. Just as she left, a shiny black Lexus pulled into the parking lot.

"Now, who could that be?" Hannah wondered out loud, and Lucy turned her head, looking out the window.

A man stepped out of the vehicle, locking it with a chirp of his key fob. He was dressed in a spotless three-piece suit and polished black dress shoes. He strode toward the bakery with an air of confidence, looking neither left nor right - a man on a mission. His hair was jet black, stylishly cut, and well-pomaded. Not a wisp of it moved out of place as he opened the door and entered the shop.

He paused, his cold, blue eyes scanning the room, taking it all in.

"Good morning. May I help you?" asked Aunt Tricia with a polite smile.

He smiled back at her, his bright white teeth a contrast to his tanned face. "May I speak to the owner, please?"

Lucy spoke up from behind him, where she still sat with her notepad.

"Hello. That would be me." She stood from the table and approached him, introducing herself with a pleasant expression. "I'm Lucy Hale. What can I do for you?" She took in his appearance, pegging him for a salesman.

His smile widened, showing perfectly even teeth. "Ms. Hale," he greeted her, inclining his head courteously. "My name is Rex Landon."

He offered his hand, and Lucy accepted it, noting that his grasp was warm and strong. They shook hands as his intense gaze connected with hers. His next words took her by surprise.

"I'd like to buy your bakery."

A STICKY TOFFEE CATASTROPHE

AN IVY CREEK COZY MYSTERY

RUTH BAKER

ALSO BY RUTH BAKER

The Ivy Creek Cozy Mystery Series

Which Pie Goes with Murder? (Book 1)

Twinkle, Twinkle, Deadly Sprinkles (Book 2)

Waffles and Scuffles (Book 3)

Silent Night, Unholy Bites (Book 4)

Waffles and Scuffles (Book 5)

Cookie Dough and Bruised Egos (Book 6)

A Sticky Toffee Catastrophe (Book 7)

Dough Shall Not Murder (Book 8)

NEWSLETTER SIGNUP

Want **FREE** COPIES OF FUTURE **CLEANTALES** BOOKS, FIRST NOTIFICATION OF NEW RELEASES, CONTESTS AND GIVEAWAYS?

GO TO THE LINK BELOW TO SIGN UP TO THE NEWSLETTER!

https://cleantales.com/newsletter/